NADINE LITTLE

Nationless Will Fall

The Faction War Chronicles 3

LITTLE PUBLISHING

Sign up for my mailing list to get a free and exclusive prequel to *The Faction War Chronicles*. Discover the explosive origins of the Faction War ten years before the events of *Captivity*. Members of my mailing list get other bonus stuff and behind-the-scenes material.

Members are also the first to hear about my new books and discounts.

Join at nadinelittle.com

'Sometimes it takes a good fall
to really know where you stand.'
Hayley Williams

'Every heart has its secret sorrows,
which the world knows not,
and oftentimes we call a man cold,
when he is only sad.'
Henry Wadsworth Longfellow, *Hyperion*

1

"Wick has another prisoner. Orders are to assemble at the screens in five minutes." The voice bounces around the cavernous space and echoes off the opaque glass of the domed ceiling.

I swallow a sigh and pack away the central computer, sealing the access panel into place. My fingertips brush the cool, shining material protecting our ultimate weapon, so close to completion.

If our inglorious leader could stop parading his victims for more than a second.

A blond head pops out of the hatch in the machine's belly, grinning at me upside-down. "Did someone say something?"

"Wick's latest video. We have to go watch."

Dylan's smile wilts. "Already? He's only had the prisoner a day."

His head disappears, replaced by his feet as he swings out of the hatch and lands beside me. Similar height, same eyes but the resemblance ends there. He got his bulk and tanned skin from Dad. Next to him, I'm a willowy goth.

Still, I'm much better looking.

"At least when we win with this we won't have to watch anymore." Dylan pats the side of the dragon, gazing up at her

1

proud head and obsidian eyes. "Indestructible killing machine. Powerful weaponry. Brain-computer whatsit."

"Interface. He's not going to stop torturing people just because we win. He'll have more to choose from."

Dylan shrugs one beefy shoulder. "Least we'll be on the winning side. Come on, let's get this over with. Pretty much quitting time, anyway."

"As your superior, I decide when it's quitting time." I smirk at him.

He laughs, slapping me on the back. I brace a hand on the dragon to stop my face from hitting her.

"And you never let me forget it."

The sky has finally cleared of grey clouds, the setting sun bronzing the muddy streets and crumbling buildings. We follow the crowd of shuffling, subdued soldiers to the nearest screen mounted on a rooftop. I fix a smile, ready to avert my gaze to a corner of the display so it'll appear as if I'm enjoying the show while avoiding much beyond blurry red and glistening pink.

I can't do anything about the screams.

The huge rectangle flickers, blackness replaced by the familiar interior of Wick's torture chamber. The reception rather than the main room, containing a large desk and stony-faced guards. The tightness in my stomach eases.

Maybe the horrific stuff will come in a later video.

The battered front door of warped plywood cants open and a prisoner is hoisted in by two of Wick's torture guards. Christine and Selena. Perky, blonde-haired twins.

And the evillest bitches I've ever met.

"She's pretty," Dylan says softly, his voice almost lost in the squelching and coughing of the people fidgeting around us.

"Not for long."

I usually avoid looking at them. I don't want their faces in my nightmares. The sounds they make are enough. Dylan is right, though—striking green eyes, a tumble of dark hair and high cheekbones. The baggy prisoner clothes don't disguise the long limbs and curves.

Pity I'm right, too.

"What faction is she from?"

"The People's Republic. She was picked up as a prisoner in Lowkirk during our attack yesterday."

Dylan raises his eyebrows. "So she went from being Revolutionary Front's prisoner to ours? That is unlucky."

"You'd know this if you didn't skive off to shag everything that moves. Yeah, you're not as clever as you think. Ill my arse."

Dylan grins, unabashed. "Oh, come on, Blake. Would you say no to Giselle? We get few comforts in this place."

I shake my head and smile.

His dereliction of duty doesn't bother me. The last thing I said to our mother before we were cut off was a promise to keep him safe. I've spent ten years protecting him. Staying in the encampment is better than going on assaults, even if I'm there.

Trying to keep myself alive is hard enough.

My smile fades as I refocus on the screen. Wick is giving the prisoner a tour, a sneer twisting his weasel-like features. Her face is pale, lips pressed together, but defiance flashes in her eyes.

The strong ones make the worst videos. Watching them fight. Watching them break. Watching them die.

I don't know which is more horrific—to become desensitised and not care anymore or to feel this awful, aching pain in my gut at the suffering of each one.

What can I do to stop it? Nothing. Rebelling against Wick would deliver me to the torture chamber and the two times I've been in there are too many. He's too strong, too well defended. Too freaking terrifying. I do what everyone does and pretend it doesn't happen. We're going to win the war. Our dragon machine will force the other factions to surrender. The thought of victory makes everything else bearable.

But what will that world be like with Wick as its leader?

I pray he returns to the man he was ten years ago. Before he got shot in the head. When he was Daniel, our party leader, not Wick, our torturer.

The video flickers, changing between cameras as the prisoner is led to the cells and propelled inside. The barred gate clangs shut behind her.

"I'm going to hurt you," Wick says, his voice soft, "so you'll wish for death. Reflect on that and the many ways I can break you."

"You fucking *bastard!*" the woman spits. The wobble in her voice ruins the strong words.

Wick leaves the cells, Christine and Selena on his heels like good pitbulls. The woman shakes the bars but they're solid iron. She slumps at the back of the cell, her head in her hands, and the screen fades to black.

"Gotta love the ones that fight."

I tense at the loud voice, my fists clenching before I can stop them. Doolly stands in a circle of his friends, his wide face split in a mean grin.

"I hope she fights when it's my turn. She won't be pretty when I'm done." His piggy eyes flick to me. "I like it when the blood gets them all slippery."

Fingers fasten around my upper arm. "Blake, don't."

I've taken a step closer, my jaw gritted tight.

"He's provoking you," Dylan says, harsh and low in my ear. "You got whipped for punching him the last time. What do you think Wick will do next? You know he's one of his favourite guards. He's not worth it."

Dylan tugs me through the dispersing crowd.

I don't shrug him off, though it's tempting. Tempting to stride up to the pig on steroids and ram my knuckles down his throat. He could break me over his knee but it didn't stop me before.

Doolly blows me a kiss. "You can tag in, O'Riley. Prove you're a real man."

"Real men don't rape women," I growl, Dylan desperately hauling on my arm, "but I guess you'd still be a virgin if you waited for someone willing, you ugly—"

Dylan yanks me around the corner of a building and out of sight of Doolly's bloated carcass.

"Fucking Christ, man, are you trying to get yourself killed?" he huffs, not relinquishing his grip. "I don't get you two. Okay, he's a repulsive delinquent. Who hangs around Wick all day and isn't? Apart from Stig, but he has no choice. Why does Doolly get to you so badly?"

I gently peel Dylan's fingers from my arm. "Excuse me if bragging about raping women offends me."

"You know it's what happens to them in there," he says. "You know worse things happen."

I know, and not only from the videos. I never told Dylan what happened that day. Doolly was there. Christine and Selena. They tried to force—

Stop thinking about it.

"But we all ignore it. We all try to forget." I glare at my boots instead of meeting Dylan's serious gaze.

"Yeah, and you suck at it. You get all sullen and snippy as soon as a new one is marched in."

"Sorry people being tortured to death also bothers me."

"We can't do anything about it."

"Can't we? We could—"

"Ssh! Fuck's sake, Blake." Dylan glances wildly at the buildings but we're alone in a narrow alleyway between two hulking factories. "Do you have a death wish? Not another word. I quite like having you as a living, breathing brother, not a mutilated corpse Wick's dumped in a ditch."

I sigh. "You're right. That was stupid. Let's stop talking about it."

We slog through the mud in silence, a long trek to the house we share on the far side of the encampment.

For the stronghold of the faction that's going to win the war, Livingston sure is depressing with its mud-slicked roads, bullet-pocked buildings and general oppressive air.

The food is crap, too.

But we built the machine. Wick took the germ of an idea and turned it into an unstoppable weapon. Shaping it like a dragon was a bit weird but she's grown on me. Seeing her come to life under my hands is amazing and flying in her... The closest I get to happy these days.

Dylan's elbow nudges me into the present. "Heads up."

A woman sits on the low wall in front of our house, surrounded by three friends who turn at our approach. Glossy chestnut hair and dewy skin make the backdrop of the house drabber. Missing tiles gape on the roof, cracks fissured through the brickwork, the garden a sad square of yellowed grass.

"Hi Blake," she says, sliding off the wall and arching her spine, her breasts thrust forward. She's changed from her jumpsuit to tight leggings and a long top cinched at her waist, emphasising her curves.

"Hi Suzanne."

Dylan puffs out his chest. Suzanne barely spares him a glance and I swallow a laugh.

"You doing anything later? Or you fancy coming round to mine for a nightcap?"

The giggle-posse titter and flip their hair. Suzanne's eyes wander down from my face and don't return.

"Another night, maybe?"

Dylan twitches.

He'd struggle to stick his chest out further and not fall over.

Suzanne pouts but it folds into a scowl. "Because you're slumming it with Rachael? How can you choose her over me?"

"Jealousy is a turn-off, Suzanne."

"Screw you, Blake."

I smirk. "Maybe another night."

She flounces off, the giggle-posse glaring at me and trailing after her in a wash of perfume and hormones.

"Are you *insane?*" Dylan hisses. "Why would you turn down Suzanne? *Suzanne.* You've fucked her before."

I don't bother scolding Dylan about his language. I'd be wasting my breath.

"Yes and, while fun, she's a lot of work. I don't have the energy tonight. I get cramp."

We walk up the broken slabs to our peeling front door. Dylan shoves it open and cocks his head.

"Can you get cramp in your penis?"

I stare at him and laughter bursts out. "Not my penis, you

idiot. There are other ways to please a woman."

The door slams, worn floorboards creaking under our boots as we troop into the living room and slump on the couch.

If we want dinner, we'll have to get up again and head to the mess hall but it seems like too much effort for tasteless glop and vitamin pills.

"I wouldn't know. I let them do all the work."

"Course you do. It's why they don't come back."

"Ass," Dylan grins, and brains me with a pillow.

2

Three days later, the dragon is complete. All tests aced. Victory over the other factions looms. When Scotland is ours, Wick plans on dominating the rest of the world, if there's enough left to dominate.

Part of me—hell, who am I kidding, every piece of me—hopes they've recovered from the internet collapse and whatever other catastrophe made them go silent, and have something more advanced to counter him.

Winning our war is one thing, enslaving the rest of the world is a whole new level of crazy dictator.

How can I escape him, live a normal life, be happy if he controls everything? The years as a member of Nationless are enough.

I try to ignore the growing claustrophobia, the panic attacks clawing me awake at night.

This is what burying your head in the sand gets you. One day you wake up surrounded by torturers, sadists and psychopaths with no way out from the mess your life has become. And no hope of forgetting the blood on your hands.

If I didn't have Dylan to keep me sane—

"Excellent work, O'Riley."

I freeze, my fingers clenching on the data logs from the

9

dragon's central computer. Paper rustles, loud in the cramped filing room. I force myself to stuff the sheets in the drawer and turn to face the cold, cold voice.

"Th-thank you, sir."

Dammit, quit stuttering!

Wick leans his long body against the door frame, blocking the exit. A strand of hair has escaped his ponytail and sticks to his cheek. My shoulders bump the filing cabinet.

"Couldn't have done it without you. The way you solved the connection problem between her operating systems…" Black eyes assess me from head to toe, lingering at places he has no business lingering. "Truly inspired."

My balls leap into my abdomen.

"I appreciate that, sir."

Oh god, leave me alone. Stop looking like you want to eat me.

"You're probably wondering why I'm here when I have someone to entertain."

I must make a small sign of surprise as his lips—too fat for his thin face—curve in a chilling smile.

"Oh, yes, she is still alive. Feeling a little rough, shall we say. I've given her the night to recover. But tomorrow—tomorrow I will break her."

I suppress a shudder, bile stinging and bitter in my throat.

The poor woman. I hope she dies quickly.

Wick steps into the room. Icy fear zips down my spine and crackles in my fingertips.

"No, I wanted to come and find you. We hardly see each other anymore."

Because I avoid you, you psychopath.

He raises his hand. My muscles tense. His fingers clasp my

shoulder, his sharp nails digging in.

"I wanted to tell you"—he bends slightly to bring his eyes level—"to keep up the good work."

He straightens and releases me. Warmth floods into my limbs.

Relief, or I've wet myself. I can't tell.

"Always a pleasure talking to you, O'Riley."

He strides out of the room and air rushes into the space. I sag against the cabinet, my skin clammy, each breath a wheeze.

"What did Wick want?"

I jump and ram my spine off the cabinet, which bangs against the wall with a clang.

"Jesus, Dylan."

"What? Are you all right? You look shiny."

"He wanted to congratulate me—a job well done," I croak.

"That's why I came to find you." Dylan pops his head out of the doorway and scans both ways. "Stig's invited us to his to celebrate. If you know what I mean."

"Great." My voice shakes only slightly. "I need a drink. Or ten."

Dylan slings an arm across my shoulders and guides me into the corridor. "Look at you, Mr Alcoholic. Though, I admit, everything tastes better when it's forbidden."

* * *

Stig's house is shabbier than ours, if possible, the walls furred with mould, dust balls the size of melons lurking under the furniture. The curtains are drawn against the copper brilliance of the sunset, the air stale.

But he makes the best moonshine.

He slumps at the scarred table in his kitchen, a smudged glass of syrupy liquid clasped in a white-knuckled fist. Bleary eyes greet us from his weathered face.

"Made this one special for you two. Poitín. To your heritage." He raises his glass. "Sláinte."

Dylan hooks a battered chair with his foot and flops into it. "You know we were born here, right?"

"Fine. To your dearly departed dad and your hopefully not departed mum." Stig hiccups, splashing the rest of his drink down his ripped, long-sleeved t-shirt.

Dad died of cancer before the independence rebellion. I've no idea what's happened to Mum, or the rest of the world. She moved to Ireland after Dad died. We've been too distracted by bombings and death to investigate the silence.

I settle myself next to Dylan, both of us facing Stig across the table.

"Seems you've given yourself a head start," I say, my smile forced.

More Dylan's friend than mine, Stig is a shambling example of what happens when you ignore your conscience. He's my age but appears decades older. An uncomfortable reminder I don't need.

"Yeah, you all right, mate? Thought this was a celebration." Dylan swipes the open bottle and pours two fresh glasses, topping up Stig's.

"What's to celebrate? Trapped in this encampment with *him*. Forced to watch…" His throat bobs. "He's ordered me to report for guard duty in the morning. Been hiding from him for days. Avoided the video screening. He sent the Hell-twins to find me."

Best not tell him Wick plans on breaking the prisoner

tomorrow.

Dylan shudders. "Fucking tough, man. But you've survived up til now. He can't punish you for much longer. Soon you'll be back on normal duties like the rest of us non-delinquents."

"He can punish me as long as he wants!" Stig says, downing his drink with a shaking hand. "I can't—I can't take it! You don't know what it's like. The videos are one thing but when it's live you get the sight and the sound and the *smell*."

The mouth of the bottle jitters against his glass, spilling liquid onto the table. I twirl my drink, my eyes watering at the fumes.

I couldn't do it. Pretending to watch the videos is as much as I can stomach.

"He rapes the men sometimes."

I jerk, alcohol slopping onto my hand. "What?"

"He rapes the men. The stronger ones. He cuts it out of the videos. Guess he doesn't want his minions to know."

The air is suddenly harder to breathe.

Oh god, if I step out of line, am slow to respond to an order, look at him funny or don't look at him at all, he'll bend me over the table in the torture chamber and—

Shut up, *shut up!*

I force myself to relax before the glass shatters in my hand. Stig attempts to refill his drink, sloshing more onto the damp table.

"Here, let me." Dylan plucks the bottle from Stig's trembling fingers and pours a measure. "It'll be all right. Just do what you normally do. Think of something else. Daydream. Forget."

"I can't. Not anymore. Can't eat. Can't sleep. I shut my eyes and see their faces. Only the drinking helps."

"Then let's fucking drink!" Dylan raises his glass, his smile a grimace. He widens his eyes at me, as though encouraging me to help lighten the mood. "To forgetting."

Stig's glass wobbles into the air.

I follow suit, trying to disguise my own tremor. "And to not going blind."

We clink glasses and down the poitín. It sears my throat and warms my belly, while no doubt dissolving my stomach lining. Coughing and choking replace the melancholy for about a second.

Stig frowns at his empty glass, his shoulders hunched low enough to disappear under the table.

"What can I do?" he whispers almost to himself. "What the hell can I do?"

"There's nothing you can do," I say, and Dylan shoots me a glare.

But it's true. There's nothing any of us can do except put our heads down, do our work and pray those black eyes never fall on us.

3

Someone pounds on the door. The noise thuds through my head and flares white. My stomach threatens to rush out my mouth. I blink at the dented clock on my bedside cabinet.

Ten am.

Jesus, I've slept in. Why did I drink so much?

I jolt upright but my legs won't hold, spilling me to the carpet in a tangle of sheets. The hammering continues.

Oh god, I'm in trouble. Wick is at the door to drag me to the torture chamber.

He'll break me alongside the woman.

I crawl into the hall instead of under the bed and totter to my feet with the aid of the wall, staggering past Dylan's room. An unintelligible curse issues from within a mound of blankets.

I'll say I'm ill. Everyone gets sick. Wick can't punish me for that.

I wobble down the stairs and glimpse myself in the cracked mirror at the bottom. White face, wide eyes, black hair stuck to my clammy forehead.

I definitely look ill.

Warped wood shudders in its frame, sending bolts of pain through my skull. I clamp my hands to my aching temples and stare at the brass doorknob. It rattles as the person outside gives it a twist. My bare feet slide backwards a step, freezing from the draught blowing in.

How long before Wick kicks the door in and hauls me through the streets in my pyjamas?

"Blake? You in there?"

My knees buckle, my palm slapping the wall to keep me vertical. A few seconds of harsh wheezing calm me enough to walk to the door. I pull it open and peer into blinding sunshine.

"Callum. Hi. What's up?"

Not Wick. One of my team. I attempt to re-swallow my heart before it flops out my mouth.

"Blake, hey! Sorry, did I wake you? You look awful. When you didn't turn up—"

My settling heart hurdles into my throat. "Does Wick know? Did he send you?"

"What? No. Wick is, um, occupied with his... You know. Should I get him instead if you're sick? There's a problem with the jet engines. Never mind, I'll—"

Callum turns. My hand shoots out but I jerk it back instead of fisting it in his collar.

"No! No, don't get Wick. I'm fine. I'll come. Just a stomach thing. Threw up. Feel better already." A smile spasms across my face.

"Um, okay." His eyes flick to me and away. "I'll head back. Meet you at the landing bay?"

"Great, yes. Thirty minutes."

I close the door and rest my forehead against it. Callum's rapid footsteps tap and fade.

The poor guy probably thinks I'm deranged.

I have to get a grip. Stupid, *stupid* mistake to get drunk with the depressive Stig and my 'let's forget and keep smiling and it'll all be okay' little brother.

If Wick or his inner circle finds out about the moonshine or my lateness…

I have to be careful. I've tried to make myself indispensable so he won't hurt me—working hard, solving problems—but he seems to admire me. And Wick's admiration is not a thing to encourage. Get him to hate me? I'll be punished.

Can't win.

I stumble upstairs. Dylan hasn't moved, only his tousled blond hair peeking from under the covers.

"I have to go in. Problem with the engines. You coming?"

He grunts.

"Take that as a no. Guess I'll see you tonight."

I sigh and slouch towards my room, willing my stomach to relax and my brain to stop battering my skull.

"Leadership's not looking so great now, is it?" comes a croak from the bed. The blankets shift enough to flash a weak grin and Dylan's greenish face.

"I hate you."

"No you don't. Mum said you have to love me."

"You make it hard. No more drinking with you and Stig."

"Uh-huh. You repeat yourself. Now go away, I need my beauty sleep."

I snort. "You need more than sleep to make you beautiful."

I dodge his tossed pillow and dart out of the doorway. A cold shower and a huge glass of water restore the rest of my spirit.

Outside, I jump into our recently serviced jeep. The sun holds a hint of warmth, drying the mud from a sucking quagmire to a trembling marsh. Few clouds mar the blue expanse of spring sky.

The landing bay is close to the domed building housing the dragon. And the torture chamber. I refuse to look at it, my fingers clenched on the steering wheel.

Hopefully, she'll be the last prisoner for a while. Wick will be too busy sacking the factions and planning world domination.

The problem with the jet engines turns out to be complex, affecting our Biofighter P-50s. Something has killed the cyanobacteria in the power cells, putting the whole line out of commission. Every microfluidic chamber needs to be replaced and restocked with fresh bacteria, which requires total disassembly of each engine. And each jet has six engines.

Technology originally from France but used in the British Army. It didn't exactly come with a manual when we stole it.

I sit on my heels and wipe my forehead on my arm. All around me, my team—minus Dylan—crouch over bio-cells stripped from the engines, surrounded by so many pieces of metal it looks like a machine has exploded. Screws, fans, shafts, ducts, nozzles. Reassembly will take *hours*.

My oil-stained fingers massage my temple.

What I wouldn't give to be at home, curled in bed, Dylan groaning in the other room. Or cajoling me into making him tea.

Rising carefully to avoid kicking an engine component out of order, I stretch my spine until it pops.

"Hey boss, can we take a break yet?"

"Yeah, we've been at it for ages, you slave-driver."

"Shocking work conditions—"

I grin at the complaints echoing through the hangar. "God, what a bunch of pussies. Fine, ten minutes."

We troop outside, swigging from recycled bottles of water tasting faintly of leaf mould. My team cluster in groups, leaning against the metal sides of the building, the sun bright on their upturned faces.

Callum sidles over to me, his ginger hair spiked with oil where he's run his hands through it. "You feeling better, Blake?"

"I am, thanks. Nothing like cyanobacteria to—"

Glass shatters, a tinkling rain of shards bursting from the domed building. The dragon springs into the sky and hovers over the encampment, her wings slicing the air, spiked tail whipping.

Beautiful. Terrifying.

"What's Wick doing?" Callum says. "Bit dramatic even for him."

My stomach drops to my feet. "That's not Wick."

"How do you—"

Two missiles burst from the concealed weapons apparatus in the dragon's flank, whooshing into the dome and destroying the structure in a slide of debris. The dragon banks towards the torture chamber, sunshine dazzling on her silver skin. Slate cracks under her clawed feet as she alights on the roof.

"That's how."

"Then who—"

"The prisoner."

How has this happened? Is Wick dead? Knocked unconscious? How, after five days of torture, did the prisoner manage to overpower him?

No one escapes.

Stone shrieks and gunfire rattles. The dragon—controlled by the woman from inside—tears at the roof of the torture chamber, blasting fire through the hole she's made.

"Boss, what should we do? Scramble the Darters?" Callum steps past me, heading for the hangar door.

I grab his arm. "No. Get to a bunker. All of you get to a bunker."

"But, sir—"

"We're not going to fight?"

"Wick would—"

I slash my hand through the air. "*Listen*. We built her to be indestructible. You fight her, you die. Get to a bunker and wait til she's gone. It's all we can do."

Mouths gape. Wide eyes flick between me and the dragon breaking the torture chamber apart, brick by flaming brick.

"Go! That's a goddamn order." I pivot on my heel towards my jeep parked on the concrete.

Tentative fingers tug at my sleeve. "You're not coming?"

"No, Callum. I've got to get Dylan. I'll see you in a bunker. Or after, if there's anything left."

"But—"

"For Christ's sake, go before she turns her attention to destroying our weapons."

My team scatters, scuttling around the hangar and out of sight. I sprint to the jeep, vaulting inside without opening the door. An RPG detonates on the side of the dragon in a puff of smoke, its trail marked by a wisp of cloud. The person who fired it is hidden from view by the buildings separating us. The dragon turns her great head.

"You idiot," I whisper through numb lips.

Lasers fire from her obsidian eyes, reducing whomever was stupid enough to take her on with a rocket to a pile of sparking fat.

The jeep's engine coughs to life. I slam it into first, the tyres scorching the concrete. A roar batters the encampment and goosebumps flare on my arms.

Our secret weapon turned against us. Certain victory to crippling loss.

Or annihilation.

I have to protect Dylan.

I floor the jeep from the landing bay, avoiding the ruin of the torture chamber. Stomping footsteps shudder into my gut. Flashes of silver race me, separated by a line of buildings. Explosions ripple, smoke belching into the sky with clods of brick.

"Please don't see me, please don't see me." I hunch over the wheel, my eyes fixed on the road ahead.

Our paths converge, her tree-trunk-thick legs swaying, splayed feet sinking into mud. I mash the brakes, swerving around. Another bowel-clenching roar. I catch movement too late. The dragon's heavy tail whistles through the air and buckles the side of the jeep. The vehicle flies sideways. A wall looms. My hands freeze to the wheel.

Dyl—

Crunch.

4

My head pounds and the ground shudders beneath me.

Why did I drink so much?

I blink stinging eyes. My mouth tastes like copper and mud. I frown at the shimmering blue sky.

Am I outside?

"Dylan!" I lurch upright and clamp my hands to my temples to hold my skull together.

The jeep lies upside-down five metres away, one wheel still spinning. Chunks of rock have scattered into the road from the building I hit. I groan and climb to my feet, bruised and battered and bleeding. The dragon is in the air not far from me, swooping and gouting flame into the streets. A battlefield separates me and Dylan, filled with burning, screaming and the sweet smell of roasted flesh.

I'll never make it to the house.

I have to try.

One step and missiles slam into a structure across the road. The hot blast plucks at my clothes. I find myself face down, choking on dirt. The dark shadow of the dragon flits overhead towards the landing bay. Metal shrieks as the hangar collapses.

I stagger through the smoke-filled streets, dodging broken, flickering screens knocked from rooftops and piles of brick

22

that were buildings. I drop to my knees in a circle of stunted bushes and yank open a hatch camouflaged as grass. Concrete steps stretch underground to a solid metal door. The hatch clangs shut behind me. Automatic lights brighten the darkness. I stumble to the bottom of the stairs and press my eye to the retinal scanner. The thick door swings open. A pale face greets me in the bunker.

Suzanne.

I have to trust Dylan is smart enough to get to safety. What else can I do? Killing myself trying to reach him helps neither of us.

Please god, let him be okay.

Too stunned to talk, I pace until the world falls silent.

* * *

There isn't much of Livingston left standing after the woman gets bored and flies off in the dragon.

I scramble out of the hatch, Suzanne squeaking, "Blake, wait!" and sprint to the bunker closest to our house. My eyes water from smoke as I skid down mounds of charred stone.

The bunker is empty.

Did no one hide? Did they all try to fight?

Morons. You can't fight death.

I run for the house, circling the street twice before recognising it. The back wall is intact, the rest a slope of rubble with a jet embedded in the middle. The dented insignia of the dragon roars at me from a rear panel.

"Dylan!" I shout and my voice cracks.

He isn't here. He wouldn't have stayed, not once he saw the dragon in the air.

Unless he put his earplugs in.

No. He's in a bunker, a different one. Or I passed him in the ruins. He'll be at the crushed remnants of the landing bay, wringing his hands and yelling my name. We'll laugh about how worried we were.

Or he's buried in our house, unable to call out.

I claw to the top of the rubble, scraping my legs on splinters of wood and exposed metal.

"Dylan?" I heave a piece of rock off the edge. Another. "Dylan?"

I call his name until I'm hoarse. Debris scatters in all directions. My nails break, bloody prints daubing each tossed stone. Blurry eyes force me to stop. I scrub my face with my dirty t-shirt and check the street.

Dylan will come skirting around the rubble and laugh at me for crying like a girl.

But I'm alone.

I resume digging, ignoring my cramping hands, the pain in my back, the dizziness. My fingertips brush a dust-coated blanket.

My bed or his?

Lifting a jagged rock, I stare into the white face of my brother, on his back in a halo of splintered wood and bedsheets.

The rock slips from numb fingers, clattering to street level.

"Dylan?" I fall to my knees and prod his chest. "Dylan, wake up."

His eyes stay shut, flecks of grit scattered on the lids. Red clumps his hair into a spike at his right temple, dried blood speckling his skin.

I fist my hand in his t-shirt and shake him. His head lolls.

I can't seem to get enough air.

Oxygen! He needs oxygen!

I press my mouth to his blue lips and puff twice. Bone grates when I pump his chest.

Why wasn't I tougher on him? I should've dragged him out of the house despite his hangover and he would've been with me. He would've been safe.

This is my fault.

No, he isn't dead. He just needs a… a defibrillator!

I shoot upright, reel, and land hard on my arse. Gritting my teeth, I rake Dylan free of the rubble and slide my hands under his armpits. I haul him backwards down the slope, losing count of how many times I fall. The sight of his pale feet bumping over the rocks almost unmans me. We reach the bottom in an avalanche of stone and dust.

My lungs burn. Each breath cuts my throat. Minutes skip away, lost to the buzzing in my head. I tug harder and trip over a rock to sprawl in the mud.

I can't get up. He's too heavy.

He's dead.

No! He needs medical care. He'll be fine.

He's been dead for hours.

I crawl to his side. "Dylan, *wake up!*"

Drops of water plop on his t-shirt, though the sky is still a perfect blue darkening towards evening. Someone makes a horrible moaning sound, a sound so lost and alone, it hurts my stomach.

I rest my head on Dylan's shattered, silent chest, and cry.

5

Stig finds me in the darkness, hunched over Dylan's body, wracked with shivers but no more tears. He flicks his fingers at the four guys behind him. I stare at their boots, not caring who they are.

None of them are Dylan.

"Come on, Blake, let go. That's it." Stig coaxes my frozen hands free of Dylan's crumpled t-shirt, talking soft and low. "We'll bring him, I promise, but we need to get you to the shelter. It's not safe out here."

Somehow, he gets me to my feet and guides me through the broken streets, the night softening the devastation of our home. I drift, limp and unresisting, the crunch of footsteps following as the men carry the body of my brother. My legs wobble but Stig's arm around my waist keeps me upright. He half-carries me down concrete steps and into a bunker. Bunk-beds cram the long, low room stretching into shadows, a few orange lights tinging the faces of the people gathered there.

They fill less than a tenth of the space built to house a thousand.

"Welcome to the survivors' club," Stig whispers, his mouth quirked as if he's making a joke. "This is all that's left."

I don't want to be here.

He steers me towards a bunk-bed in the corner. I collapse onto the edge of the mattress. He tugs my boots off and I let him.

"Lie down, Blake." Still the soothing voice, as if I may break and start screaming.

Maybe I will. Later. My mouth is glued shut, my throat crushed. My eyelids rasp with each blink.

I flop backwards. Stig tucks the covers around me, his face even more creased. He hisses at the sound of approach and tells someone to leave me alone.

It suits me. I just want to die.

Time becomes snippets of colour and pain and hushed voices. I sleep or pass out. What does it matter? Awake, I fix my eyes on the metal slats of the bunk above mine and try not to feel. I eat what's offered without tasting it, drink everything handed to me without it easing the tightness in my throat. People talk but I don't answer, unable to focus on their faces because it hurts to know it won't be the person I want to see.

It will never be the person I want to see.

I shut my stinging eyes. Listening to the voices around me is preferable to the shrieking inside my skull.

"We need to send a runner to get help, warn the others. Bathgate, Avoncraig and Harbrax should be enough. Any volunteers?"

"I'll do it."

Dependable Callum, always so eager to assist. The only one of my team to survive. I hate him for that. Why does he get to live?

Conversations merge.

"Why would you bring him in here? Take him out and dump him with the others." The furious screech bounces between the bunk-beds.

I turn my head, slow, stiff. A body lies inside the door, surrounded by people. Long, charred limbs, dirty t-shirt and briefs. The crowd shifts to show his face.

What's left of his face.

Bone flecks a maroon concavity, Wick's brown hair in disarray.

Did falling rubble do that? What happened in those last few moments in the torture chamber? No one seems to have questioned Stig despite him being the guard on duty. I could ask him but the words float somewhere, lost between my chest and my brain.

"Let's burn him," a woman giggles.

Karen? Keira? Who the hell cares?

She claps her hands to her mouth, her eyes darting to the assembled people as if Wick will jump out.

But he's dead, as are all his willing torture guards. The only bright spot in the darkness. No Doolly. No Hell-twins.

No Dylan. No Rachael, either. Our relationship was in the exciting early stage. I liked her shyness, so different to the women who look at me like I'm something to eat.

Rachael didn't deserve to die. Dylan didn't deserve to die.

I turn my face to the wall. Minutes, hours—days?—pass.

Suzanne slithers into the bed, her moist breath in my ear. "I know what will make you better."

She presses my hand to her breast, her nipple hard under my palm. Her lips nuzzle my throat, leaving a trail of wetness. I blink at the slats above me.

There are ten in total, evenly spaced, a crisp edge of white visible where the sheet is tucked under the mattress.

Suzanne releases my hand to cup my face and slobber on my

mouth. "Come on, Blake, you're the only one who can make me feel good. Here, I'll make it easy."

She wriggles up the bed and plants a knee on either side of my head.

"What in god's name are you doing?"

Suzanne yelps and tumbles off, landing on her arse on the floor and scowling at Stig. "What's it got to do with you? I'm cheering him up."

"By molesting him? For Christ's sake, Suzanne—"

"Molesting him?" she sputters. "Well, of course you wouldn't know what making love looks like."

"Are you blind? He's practically comatose. He's in no condition to 'make love' to anybody."

She scrambles to her feet, her cheeks flushed, and jabs a finger into Stig's chest. "You're just jealous because I won't sleep with you."

"Jealous, sure. Because all anybody is thinking about now is whether they can get in your pants."

"Well, save yourself the bother. It'll never be you, you—you *geriatric*." She sticks her nose in the air and flounces off.

"Scathing as ever, Suzanne," Stig yells. He fusses with the covers over my chest. "Sorry about that, Blake. Took my eyes off her for a second. She's been circling you like a bloody shark."

I don't respond to his dry laugh. He squeezes my shoulder and drifts away. After a period of staring at the slats above me, moaning comes from the back of the room.

"Yes, that's it!" Suzanne gasps.

It sounds forced and continues for an age with no change of inflection or sign of climax. People congregate nearer the door, their eyes flicking to the shadows.

"What are you doing?" Suzanne hisses. "Did I tell you to stop?"

The moaning resumes.

Poor guy probably has lockjaw.

My lips twitch.

"Can you get cramp in your penis?"

Dylan's voice slides a spear into my chest.

I'll never hear it again, never see him again. Never laugh about stupid, immature crap with him again. Where is his body? What time is it? What *day* is it? Has he been dumped in the rubble to be pecked by crows? Eyes like mine plucked out—

I explode to my feet. The sheets tangle my ankles and I fall to my knees, my palms slapping the smooth floor.

"Blake!"

"Are you all right?"

"Here, let me help—"

I shrug off the clinging hands and wobble upright, staggering for the door on weak legs. I tug at the handle, forgetting it needs a fingerprint scan to unlock it. Pale faces gape at me, whispers fluttering like dried, blown leaves.

"Hey, Blake, buddy, what you doing?" Stig says, sidling around to stand beside me, his hands held out.

"I need to bury him," I say, yanking at the door, my hair falling into my eyes. "I need to bury Dylan."

"Okay, we can do that, but not right now—"

"No! I can't leave him. I can't let him rot out there. *Why won't this fucking thing open!*"

My scream bounces off the ceiling. People wince and glance at each other.

Stig pats the air near my arm, not quite touching. "It's only the second day, Blake."

I stop jerking at the door.

Two days? Only two days? It feels like goddamn *years*.

"He'll be okay until tonight. That's when we'll bury him, all right? It's daylight. Too dangerous. You know other factions always scavenge the wreckage."

They'll desecrate his body.

I shoulder Stig from the control panel. He stumbles, his eyes wide.

"I can't leave him out there." My fingers stab at the scanner. "I can't leave him alone. I want to see him. Bring him in here. Keep him safe. I need—"

Stig grabs my wrist. We wrestle, our jaws clenched. He pulls me back from the door into a semi-circle of worried faces. I twist my wrist free and shove him hard. He sprawls on the floor with a startled yell. I whirl for the control panel.

"Stop him!"

Hands grip my arms. My finger slips off the scanner before it can complete the process. Rage slices claws into my chest. My boots and fists lash out. People twitch away, clutching bleeding faces and bruised shins. I jam my finger on the scanner. A light turns green. The door lock thunks free. My fingers curl on the handle. An arm throttles me from behind and the world becomes a swirl of colour. My spine hits the floor, bodies tumbling on top, pinning me and panting into my face.

"No!" I shout, bucking underneath the crushing weight. "Let me go! I have to see him. I want to see my brother!"

I struggle. Someone makes a shushing noise in my ear as if calming a frightened horse. Heat pulses from my skin. I try to bite the people within reach and hands clamp my head still.

"Please! I want Dylan. I want my brother. I want—"

Stig appears above the scrum of bodies. I have trouble focusing on his face.

"It's all right, Blake. Everything's going to be all right." Cool fingers brush my forehead. "Sorry about this, buddy."

There's a sharp pain in my neck. Shadows soften the frantic anger. The suffocating weight is removed and I float off towards the ceiling.

6

Rain batters my head and plasters my hair to my face. My brittle fingers grip a curved piece of metal. Globs of mud splatter everywhere, covering the clothes moulded to my body, swirling in my boots that are sinking into sludge, difficult to see in the darkness in the bottom of the hole. The scrape of metal and the pounding rain drown my harsh breathing.

I'll keep digging until everything goes black. Until I'm too deep to feel, to care.

"That's probably enough, Blake. Blake? *Blake!*" Stig crouches at the edge, level with my head, and shakes my shoulder. "Climb out, now."

I took a swing at him when he tried to help me dig Dylan's grave. I'll be guilty later when I'm something other than rage and sorrow.

Everyone else is avoiding me since my slight meltdown, tip-toeing past with worried glances, as if I might leap up and rip their throats out. Stig forced two guys to accompany us as guards.

No one else came to say goodbye.

Pale fingers wiggle in front of my face. "Take my hand. I'll pull you out."

The makeshift shovel splashes in the water pooled at the

bottom of the hole. The level reaches my ankles, the surface roiling beneath the lashing rain.

"Bury me with him."

Stig's hand bruises my shoulder. "Don't be ridiculous. Dylan wouldn't want that."

"Dylan's not here."

"Blake, get your ass out of that hole before I drag you out."

I snap my head up, ready to snarl at him but sadness deepens the lines on his face.

He loved my brother, too.

Mud oozes between my fingers on the slippery edge. I jump, my boots scraping the sides but my arms shake too much to support my weight. I land on my arse in icy water, blinking up at Stig through rain-blurred eyes.

"Might—need you to—drag me out—after all," I say between chattering teeth.

He stretches his arm towards me. I lever free of the mire and Stig holds my hand while the other two guys pull him backwards, hoisting my body from the grave. I wobble to my feet to stand at the edge and stare into the pit. Stig stays beside me, probably to stop me from toppling in. The others bring the shape wrapped in spare bedsheets, a package too small to be my foul-mouthed, cocky little brother.

Maybe it isn't him. Maybe he isn't dead.

Stig's fingers clamp on my upper arm. The two men lower Dylan into the grave, water and mud staining his shroud. I find myself on my knees without any memory of how I got there. My hand fists the two pairs of dog-tags under my drenched fleece, one my own. The words on the other brand my palm.

O'Riley, Dylan. Nationless, Livingston.

What do I have to live for now?

Stig's arm wraps around my back.

"I'm so sorry, Blake. So sorry." His choked voice whispers it over and over.

The sludge claims my brother. Each heavy shovelful slaps into the grave, each a punch to my stomach. Our two guards step back, mud to their elbows, their eyes darting to the darkness beyond our lanterns.

I scrub my face, placing a hand on the slick grave mound. "They'll pay for this."

"Who will?" Stig eases away, the wetness emphasising his bony shoulders.

"Anyone from The People's Republic."

"It's hardly their fault."

I glare at him. He stands up and slides out of reach.

"Fine, but that's where she came from. The one goddamn woman who did all this and murdered my brother. I want all of them to hurt, like I hurt. They deserve that at least."

Stig opens his mouth. Closes it. I shove to my feet and he takes another step backwards.

"Wick hurt her," he mumbles, his eyes dropping.

"And she killed him, didn't she? Battered his face. The rest of us did nothing. I felt *sorry* for her!" Water and mud splatter from my gesturing finger. "She should have taken the dragon and left us alone. We suffered under Wick's terror for years. She can't cope for five days? Five days before she scurries back to Calders to recover and be pampered. The conquering hero. Bet she's already bragging about it."

Loathing bubbles in my gut. It's better directed at her than hollowing me out.

I'll probably never see her again.

But if I do, I hope she fights me. I'll wrap my fingers around her throat, and squeeze.

We slog to the bunker in silence, our shoulders stooped against the relentless torrent. Whispers chase our sloshing footsteps through the long room to the bathrooms off the rear corner. My anger dulls, replaced by exhaustion. I stutter to a stop in the narrow corridor, staring at the muddy puddle collecting beneath my boots.

"Blake, where… Oh. Come on. A little further. You need to get out of those wet clothes and warm up."

I hate his soft voice, the gentle note of persuasion. Hate being treated like an invalid.

Hate him for surviving.

He coaxes me into the blue-tiled shower area, each one enclosed in an opaque cubicle. Low stone benches run between the rows. He guides me away from the doorway and opens a shower near the end of the first row, twisting the water on. My frozen fingers fumble with the zip of my fleece. Stig tries to help but I bat at his hands.

He rolls his eyes. "Punch me if it makes you feel better but I'm undressing you and putting you in that shower before you catch pneumonia."

"You sound like my mother."

"Good. So stop being a baby and let me take your clothes off."

I manage a smirk. "Never knew you felt that way about me."

A tightness in his face relaxes, smoothing some of the lines around his eyes. "As great a privilege as it may be to see you naked, I prefer women."

He holds his hands out towards my zip and cocks an eyebrow.

I sigh. "Fine. Do it. My stupid fingers don't work, anyway."

"You concede with such grace."

Is this how he was with Dylan? I only ever saw him crippled by his conscience, stress bowing his spine and thinning his hair as he shuffled from one place to the next. He seems calmer despite our situation. Is it Wick's death? The destruction of the torture room?

He strips me of my sodden clothes, leaving me shivering in my boxer shorts.

"You can take those off yourself once you've warmed up. We're not that close."

"I can see why my brother liked you."

A shadow flits across his face. He busies himself gathering my clothes.

"Dylan would want me to make sure you're okay. Until help comes."

A waft of steam billows from the open shower, masking Stig's expression.

The showers in the bunker seem hotter than the tepid splutter of the ones aboveground.

"You going somewhere after that?"

He smiles but it leaves his eyes sad. "Who knows where any of us will end up."

A violent shiver forces me into the warmth of the shower. Stig disappears out of the door, the hiss of water swallowing his whisper.

It sounds like, "Forgive me."

7

I sleep the rest of the night and the whole of the next day, dreaming of Dylan. Games we played as kids. Girls we chased. Our proper fight when we liked the same one—I bloodied his lip, he kneed me in the balls. She tried to have us both and we decided such dishonesty wasn't worth it.

Bros before… Well, you know.

I dream of the day he appeared at my door and begged me to come home. The frantic call from Mum when travel became impossible and he was stranded. My confident promise. My selfish happiness at having him with me instead—

A metallic clang jerks me awake to the muted orange glow of the bunker. A bedraggled figure stumbles through the door and collapses to their knees. I tense to throw back the covers but Stig reaches them first.

"Callum! Jesus, what happened?"

Callum turns his face into the light. One half is swollen and weeping, like his skin has been scoured. His clothes are ragged, torn at the knees and charred at the edges.

"They're gone—we're done—we can't—"

He bows his head and sobs, his scratched hands hiding his face. The survivors' club gathers around him, all shuffling feet and anxious voices. I stay in my warm nest of sheets, my heart beating fast.

"Who's gone, Callum? What did you see?" Stig speaks in the same soft voice he uses on me, one hand squeezing Callum's heaving shoulder.

"R-Revolutionary Front," Callum gulps. "They attacked."

"Who? Harbrax? Avoncraig?"

Callum shakes his head. I fist my hands to keep myself from screaming at him to spit it out.

"Us. They attacked Nationless. All our encampments are gone." His voice dissolves in tears. "Help isn't coming."

Cries of horror flit around the room. Stig staggers to his feet and sags against the nearest bunk-bed, his pale face ashen.

"No," he whispers almost to himself. "This wasn't meant to happen."

What part *was* meant to happen, exactly?

I swallow hard to keep from vomiting. A desperate hopelessness threatens to suck me under.

What the hell are we supposed to do now? Stay in the bunker until the war ends? It could take years. Plead sanctuary with another faction? They'll shoot us on sight. Stumble around in no man's land? Something out there will eat us.

I bite my lip to quiet my frantic breathing.

This is a nightmare. I'm still asleep. If I shut my eyes really tight, I'll wake up in my own bed, Dylan snoring in the room across from mine. None of this is real. How can it be? How could the strongest faction be obliterated in only three days?

Other weeping joins Callum's. Stig's face couldn't get any greyer. Several people fall to their knees, pulling at their hair, their mouths stretched wide.

"No!" Stig shouts. "This doesn't mean we're dead. This isn't the end. Look at where we are. We're safe as long as we stay in the bunker."

"But it's only stocked for a few weeks," comes a wobbly voice from the shadows. "It's not meant to be lived in forever. We'll run out of food."

Stig shoves away from the bunk-bed, almost overbalancing. He paces in front of the huddled Callum.

"It's stocked for a thousand, it'll last a few months. And—and we'll scavenge the other bunkers! That'll keep us going for *years!*"

"Revolutionary Front has probably cleared them out, or The People's Republic," the same voice argues.

I grit my teeth at the name.

This is their fault. *Her* fault.

"They don't know where the bunkers are. They might have stumbled across some but most will be intact. We have to do it tonight. We have to gather everything we can from the other bunkers and hole up in here until—"

"Until what?" Suzanne says, striding forward. "Didn't you hear? No one's coming."

"Well what do you suggest? Mass suicide?"

She scowls and crosses her arms, her breasts straining against her navy shirt, the top buttons undone and flashing her cleavage. "I *suggest* you stop acting like our leader or something."

"Why? You got a better idea? Please, Suzanne, tell us what you think we should do?"

Her eyes spark. The silence stretches, interrupted by quiet sobs.

"I think—we should gather—as much food as possible—from the other bunkers." She growls the words as if they're painful.

"Great. Glad we agree." Stig swivels to the desolate people

clustered on the floor. "Right, everyone, let's split into groups of ten."

Somehow, he cajoles them to their feet, a wild enthusiasm twisting his face. He counts them off into ten groups. They shuffle together as if they're about to be led to the gas chamber.

"What about Blake?" Suzanne says.

Stig's eyes hesitate on me. "I'll stay with Blake."

"How does he get to mope around doing nothing?"

Mope around? *Mope!*

I'm beginning to realise Suzanne is a colossal bitch. I should have known. Like most beautiful women, her lovely shell disguises a screeching harpy.

"Jesus Christ, Suzanne, he lost his brother."

"So what? We've all lost someone. We've all lost everything!"

I guess she has a point.

Muttering under her breath, she leaves with the rest. Stig watches them go, the hush settling in the corners. The life drains from his face at the closing of the door, years marking his skin in the space of a few seconds. He helps the still sobbing Callum limp to a bed close to me and tucks him in. His dull eyes meet mine.

I clear my throat. "I could have gone. I'm, well, not fine exactly but not comatose."

A smile zips across his face, gone in a blink. "Better to rest while you can. This news, plus Dylan, it's more than most people could bear."

"I'm not exactly holding up great."

"Promise me something?"

"What?"

"You won't give up."

"What do you mean?"

"Dylan would want you to live. Promise me you'll try to live. To find something more than this." He spreads his arms, indicating the desolate bunker or maybe the shattered ruin of our home above.

The wider devastation of our faction.

I swallow before speaking. "What about you?"

"Don't worry about me. Just promise me. For Dylan."

"I was never going to kill myself. I might have gone a little crazy..." I trail off at his intense gaze. "Okay, I promise."

He turns on his heel. "All right, then."

"Wait. Where are you going?"

"I need to be alone for a minute."

He pauses at the door to the bathrooms as if he may say something else but he continues through. I frown at the slats.

What was that about? What does it matter if I live? There's nothing left anymore. Though Stig is right—Dylan wouldn't want me to give up, no matter how terrible the situation.

A shining beacon of optimism, my brother.

I picture his face, smirking at me while he calls me a pussy. He'd turn it into a competition, betting he'd live longer if he were here.

"You haven't beaten me yet, little brother," I whisper.

Brilliant. I'm talking to myself. The insanity begins.

But it's comforting to imagine him with me, if only for a second.

I kick the covers off and sit on the edge of the bed, running my fingers through my hair so it falls in my eyes and tickles my cheeks.

Dylan always said it made me look like Mum—feminine and delicate.

The douche.

I stand and stretch.

I feel rested if nothing else. Maybe, in a few decades, I'll be happy again. Though how I'm going to survive, stuck in a bunker with—

The gunshot seems loud in the empty space. My knife appears in my hand without me having to think about it.

Only Wick's guards got the guns.

"Stay here," I direct at Callum who's trying to fight from a tangle of sheets, the tears still shiny on his face.

I jog to the door leading to the bathrooms and press my shoulder to the wall, peering around the frame. The corridor stretches empty.

I don't need to whisper Stig's name, I know what I'll find. No enemy can access the locked bunker. Callum, Stig and I are the only ones here.

Blood splatters the tiles of the shower room, bright against the blue, a hint of copper tainting the air. His limp hand clutches a Browning at his side, fallen from where he shoved it in his mouth, his lips stained black. Apart from that, he could almost be sleeping. Well, that and the halo of red, grey and flecks of white behind his lolling head. A thick rivulet weaves between the tiles towards a drain in the centre of the floor.

I should have made him promise, too. Why does he get the easy way out?

A footstep scrapes in the corridor. I whirl, my blade up. Callum yelps and stumbles against the wall, clutching a sheet around his shoulders. Drying scabs ooze fresh blood down his raw cheek.

"Jesus, Callum. Now is not the time to sneak up on me."

"S-sorry, Blake. Wanted to check you were okay." He edges forward and I can't block him from the sight through the doorway. His one good eye widens. "So he lied, then. He knew it was hopeless."

"It's not hopeless."

"Stig looks pretty hopeless."

"Stig wrestled with his own demons. You know that."

He shakes his head and hobbles away. "We all have demons. We all have regrets. Maybe Stig's right—why fight it for a few months of scraping by? What kind of life is that?"

"Callum…"

He disappears through the door. I sigh and turn to Stig.

"And how's this supposed to help me, you selfish git?" I stop short of kicking him. "You think I wouldn't care if you died, too? If you left me here alone with these idiots?"

A black hole gapes beneath my feet, a seductive voice whispering for me to fall in. It would be so easy. No more fighting, no more pain. A bleak, cold darkness before oblivion. Let myself waste away—

Quit it.

I stomp into the long room and yank covers off the nearest bed. I spread them on the chilled tile floor and plant a boot on either side of Stig, sliding my hands under his armpits.

"Don't you dare dribble on me or you're getting dumped in the incinerator," I say through gritted teeth, peeling him off the wall and pivoting to waddle onto the sheets with him slithering between my legs.

Anger is preferable to mourning. I'm wrung out. If I look in the mirror, I'll see the ravaged face and bleary eyes of an old man.

Like Stig, in the end.

I lower him onto the sheets. A piece of something plops, splattering red on the pristine white. I swallow hard and taste something similar to the sea.

Do brains smell like salt water?

I march into the corridor and gasp recycled air. The urge to gag or faint subsides. I tug Stig's Browning from his stiff grip and tuck it into my waistband then wrap the sheets tight and hoist him onto my shoulder. He doesn't weigh much though he's taller than me.

He's practically emaciated.

I carry him into the long room, telling myself I'm imagining warm blood splattering the backs of my legs. Callum huddles on his bed, no part of him visible beneath the mound of covers. The thick door unlocks with a thud. I almost drop Stig on the stairs, struggling to open the hatch. His body seems heavier.

The night air strokes my skin and ruffles my hair. I pause to listen. No voices, no scrape of stone. A tattered cloth flaps from the top of some rubble. The distant call of an owl is mournful and lost.

I avoid the squelching mud, walking on chunks of rock and fractured concrete, Stig jiggling on my shoulder. The skeleton of a building floats out of the dark, the doorway a blacker shape.

"So help me god, Stig, if you get me killed…"

What am I going to do, haunt him? Find him in hell and shout at him?

I ease into the building, the gun loose in my hand. Nothing attacks me out of the shadows. Something scurries away but I force my legs onward and lower Stig onto the shattered floor in a tiny space clear of rubble. Ten minutes later, stones cover his body.

I sway over the jagged cairn.

Dylan owns my grief. I have nothing for everyone else.

"I hope it was worth it," I whisper, and stumble into the dark.

8

Ten more people die that night. The closest groups report growling, screaming. And wet ripping sounds when the screaming stopped.

Abominations. Creatures we created and lost control of.

They like the night best.

The raid on the bunkers has limited success. Most are buried under rubble. Several have been found and looted or wrecked by animals. The haul from the rest will last a few months.

The dire mood worsens at the news of Stig's suicide. Even Suzanne seems shocked. People cower in their beds, anguished sobbing more common than stilted conversation.

I hate it. Their misery suffocates me, compounding my own until it's hard to breathe, to think. To feel anything but despair. I hate them for it. They're alive, what right do they have to weep? I'd give anything for Dylan to be here, shaken but still trying to bolster everyone's spirits.

On the fifth day, I can't stand it anymore. I have to get out before I hurt someone.

I pull on navy combats and a t-shirt, fastening Stig's holster around my waist and slipping a knife into my boot. No one protests as I unlock the door. Callum raises his head but says nothing, the swelling on his face reduced enough to open both eyes.

I hop up the steps and slip out of the hatch. It clangs behind me. I wince but nothing moves in the rubble. No enemies, no ravenous creatures.

Just me and the dead.

I jog through the wreckage, glad for the exercise. The air tastes sweet in comparison to the stuffy oppression of the bunker. The sun warms my face and my stride lengthens. I focus on my heartbeat, on the wind rushing in my ears, the blood reawakening neglected muscles.

For a moment, I feel almost free.

Then I trip over a severed leg.

I sprawl on my face. Blood wells on my palms and stings in the shallow scrapes. I crawl from the stink of rot and lean against a fractured concrete pillar.

Reckless. What would Dylan say?

He'd probably challenge me to race him to the boundary without chickening out.

My fingertips rub my aching chest but it's an internal pain.

A pain I'll always have.

I shove to my feet in a swirl of dust.

The bunker is safe. Better to stay in it and try not to go crazy than run out and get shot. Maybe we won't be cooped up for long. The People's Republic have our dragon. They could crush the rest in weeks.

My nails dig into my throbbing palms.

They don't deserve the victory. They didn't slave for years to build her. Sacrifice their integrity for a brilliant leader who became brilliantly insane. Ignore the terrible things done in their name. Live in constant fear.

They didn't have to pray that winning would make it all

worth it.

I glance at the sky for a flash of silver among the clouds, a spurt of flame and a stomach-clenching roar.

Will they show us mercy? Or will the woman who stole the dragon delight in personally torturing us?

Violence breeds hatred, not forgiveness.

I skirt a huge pile of stone that was a munitions factory, shards of brass glinting in the sun. A scream scares a flock of crows pecking at the rubbish. I hold my breath.

The voices are too far away to understand the words.

I creep closer between piles of rubble, heading in the direction of the bunker. A wide space of scattered red bricks opens up. The hatch gapes, a crowd gathered around it. A Raider-3 tank hulks over everything, black and forbidding, the charging portals of the double-barrelled proton cannons glowing blue. Smaller vehicles sit nearby—jeeps, Centipedes, an ancient Vector patrol vehicle. A man stands with his back to me, his tawny hair artfully mussed, a fist bunched in the collar of Callum's shirt.

"So this is where you scuttled off to. How many are left?" The man shakes his arm and Callum wobbles in his grip, his ravaged face turning purple.

John Anders. Second in command of Revolutionary Front, leader in his own mind. And an annoying arsehole who loves the sound of his own voice. He would've been the one who rallied his troops to destroy the rest of our encampments.

The smug expression he must've had…

We didn't even kill his stupid party leader, though he blames us for it.

I scrape my nails into the dirt instead of my aching palms.

There's nothing I can do. Twelve bullets and a knife won't

kill half of them.

Callum chokes and scrabbles at John's hands. "It—it's only me. No one else."

Oh god, did he come looking for me, wanting to make sure I wasn't in trouble?

John laughs. "Well, in that case, you're not much use."

He pulls an ivory-handled knife from a holster at his waist and rams the blade into Callum's stomach. Callum's eyes widen, a horrible whine in his throat. John jerks his arm up and pivots away. Glistening intestines spill from the wound in a tangle of pink and red. Callum drops to his knees then onto his face.

"Bury the bunker." John twirls his blood-stained knife in the air. "Search the rest. I want no Nationless scum left alive."

The Raider-3 trundles forward, stone shrieking and exploding to dust under its tracks. The proton cannons aim into the open hatch. A blinding flash, and a whump vibrates through my boots. Rock fountains upwards. Ozone sears my nose. The tank fires again, and again, its massive bulk jerking backwards.

What does it sound like to the survivors' club huddled below? How will they react when they realise what's happened? The food will last a few months but then they'll die. Trapped. Will they turn on each other? Commit suicide rather than starve? Or will they eat the weakest, any atrocity acceptable if it means living a little longer?

We were trained by Wick after all.

A sickening shiver cramps my gut.

Thank god. Thank god I wasn't with them.

The soldiers spread out from the wreckage of the hatch, several jumping into vehicles and zooming into the dust. The rest sweep their rifles over the pulverised stone, moving slowly in a line. I skitter away, using the charred ruins for cover, and sprint for the boundary of the encampment, no destination in mind.

No plan but putting distance between me and John's army.

I reach the boundary fence after half an hour, a stitch sinking teeth into my side, the taste of blood in my mouth. The metal fence posts are surprisingly intact, black laser-cameras perched on top. No wires stretch between, the fence composed of particle beams forming an impenetrable barrier.

But not today. No power to the fence, no shimmering beams.

I hold my shaking hand close to be safe but no heat caresses my palm.

I dart through into no man's land.

9

Sweeping spotlights paint the encampment a ghostly grey.

Calders, stronghold of The People's Republic.

Is she down there, tucked in bed, comfortable and safe? She managed to wield the dragon with devastating efficiency, she can't have been that injured. I picture her content smile and the anger burns my gut. I bet she's snuggled up with Marshall, her leader. No way someone that pretty isn't in the harem of women he pampers and shags. His Elite Guard. Wick said Marshall bragged about them on the comms system. She was probably one of the first to sleep with him. Anything for an easier life.

Is there a woman alive who doesn't use sex for personal advancement or as a weapon? A tool to manipulate the weakness of men.

Wind sighs through the leaves of the trees behind me. I scan the darkness between the trunks, my heart hammering, but nothing moves.

I stand on a cliff overlooking a wide, flat valley, Calders in the centre, some miles from my position.

I can't risk going closer and encountering a patrol or a laser-camera on their boundary fence. It'd melt my face since I'm not on their database.

It took me a day to reach Calders. Stunned at the loss of the bunker, I'd lingered on the outskirts of Livingston until Revolutionary Front left and night fell. I went back in, jumping at every sound, gun clutched tight in my hand. I barely recognised where the bunker had been. Rubble obliterated the open space, tonnes of it burying my remaining comrades and leaving me alone.

The last survivor of Nationless.

I forced myself away instead of pressing my ear to the ground in the hope of hearing their voices. There was some comfort in knowing they were down there.

They'll probably live longer than me.

I scavenged a few paltry items from the wreckage: dented food tins, a couple of packs of dehydrated spaghetti bolognaise, a lighter, spare clothes, a small first aid kit and some cooking utensils. My worldly possessions, along with my weapons. They hang on my back, wrapped in a dirty sheet.

I stare at The People's Republic—haughty, strong, secure—and hate them so much I want to attack. To run at their fence and hurt them. But I can do nothing.

They will never pay for what they've done.

I bow my head and turn away before I do something stupid. A branch snaps in the tangled darkness. Silvery light from the moon reflects off a shifting pair of eyes. My breath catches in my throat. I raise my gun and slide backwards a step.

What kind of abomination is it? One of our own—freaking cyborg lynxes with metal talons—or some genetically spliced monster?

It growls, flashing sharp teeth, a wrinkled muzzle and wiry hair. The position of its glowing eyes suggests its head will reach my stomach.

The perfect height for ripping out my intestines.

I squeeze the trigger. The gunshot batters the night and I sprint in the opposite direction, following the line of the cliff as it descends into the valley. Loose rocks roll under my boots, twisting my ankles and threatening to pitch me over the edge. Branches whip my face, their claws cloaked by the black. I tangle myself in a patch of brambles and some kind of huge bush, wasting several frantic minutes thrashing and wheezing, the thorns biting my skin. I yank free, leaving most of my flesh, and reach the valley floor, plunging into rank agricultural pasture. Moonlight casts my shadow on a field of clustered flowers gleaming in the dark like a blanket of snow. A pungent mustard stink rises from the plants, almost too thick to breathe.

I stumble into a deserted village somewhere south of Calders, gasping, exhausted, my sheet of possessions bruising my spine. Ivy chokes the brickwork, trees growing between and slowly crumbling the buildings. I select one at random, the rotten front door canted on its hinges. The stairs to the upper level creak under my weight but don't collapse. I barricade myself in a room and slump in the corner, sweating, shaking, trying not to sound like I'm suffering an asthma attack.

Two nights in no man's land, one abomination attack, one bullet down. At this rate, I'll be out of ammo in less than a month.

Then I'll be dead.

10

How do I survive the first month? Luck, stubbornness, a ludicrous desire to live? I wake each day chilled, damp and stiff, hunger hollowing my gut. Burdock, pignuts and clover relieve the ache but I crave protein. Hunting is difficult without using my gun, my snares and traps laughable. I relent and shoot a deer, so starving I eat it raw and immediately throw up.

I stay in the abandoned village for a week, only leaving the room to forage and collect the pots I scattered outside for rainwater. Otherwise, I stare at a patch of wall and imagine Dylan is with me, mocking my limp snares and telling me to take a bath or no woman will ever sleep with me again. Sometimes, I find myself talking to him aloud, whole conversations we've had before or ones I would've had, given the chance.

It's slightly worrying, but no one else is there to stop me going crazy.

Mornings and evenings are the worst. Mornings because I hope to discover it's all a nightmare. Loneliness hits in the evenings.

The days are filled with fighting to live.

I move on when a ferocious battle startles me awake in the middle of the night. Distant explosions, gunfire and screams roll across the landscape. Flashes of laser fire and blinding white light brighten the sky towards Calders. I wait, gritty-eyed, my heart tripping in the dark, and pray the skirmish doesn't come closer.

When the fighting stops, I pack my meagre belongings and return to my vantage point on the cliff, guided by the stink of rot from the carcass of the beast I shot.

Nice to know blind terror didn't affect my aim.

The valley opens below me, a palette of violet and orange and blue against the dawn. A pall of smoke hangs over Calders. What's left of Calders. There's a scattered, irregular circle of blasted rock and burning rubble. No buildings left standing.

Reminds me of Livingston.

How the hell did this happen? Where is the dragon?

Squadrons of soldiers march through the wreckage, a battalion of vehicles ringing the boundary. It's too far to tell what faction they belong to. Who I should be thanking.

I hope it isn't John. I hate that guy.

A snigger tickles my throat.

Christ, the woman really is unlucky—surviving torture, returning a hero to be blasted to pieces and buried in the ruins of her home.

Justice.

I sit hard on my arse and shake with laughter. My stomach aches, tears blurring my eyes. The fierce joy turns to crying between one breath and the next and I sob into my knees, my arms wrapped around my legs.

A pretty tragic picture.

The sun tinges the land golden by the time I quit weeping and wobble to my feet. My dry throat clicks, my eyes swollen, chest carved out.

This grief business really sucks.

I brand the sight of Calders reduced to ash in my mind for when I need a spirit booster and start walking south-east away from The People's Republic, away from the factions.

It's too volatile to stay in the no man's land between territories. Better to risk the no man's land of the Borderlands.

My filthy, ragged clothes, desperate expression and questionable hygiene will fit right in.

* * *

I keep on the move for two weeks, the constant vigilance and changing scenery helping to distract me. I sleep in trees to avoid being munched, though it's never comfortable and always cold. I fall a few times, bruising my shoulder and gashing my head, warm blood trickling to my chin as I blink stupidly at the grass.

Mornings aren't so bad anymore. It's hard to trick myself when I wake with a faceful of leaves and branches poking my spine. I despise the nights, listening for the rustle of creatures prowling through the undergrowth, their claws scraping bark as they try to reach me.

I probably smell delicious to them. Sweat, old blood and fear. Yum.

Drinking becomes a problem. Rainwater only goes so far. Watercourses and reservoirs were a target for bioweapons. Most are still toxic and with no way to safely test... I stumble around in a lush, wet land, my tongue so dry it cracks, each swallow painful. Chewing on wood sorrel alleviates the thirst a little but the constant dehydration short-circuits my intelligence.

I waste two bullets on a deer. It bounds into the trees, the white flash of its tail mocking me. I shoot a third bullet after it out of pure frustration. My next bullet kills a wild sheep, a scrawny beast with twigs and thorns tangled in its fleece. I drink its blood, like sucking on metal, and fight not to puke. The meat is tough, gamey, but wonderful. I stuff chunks of fleece inside my clothes at night for extra warmth.

If anyone wants to find me, they can follow the puffs of white I scatter in my wake.

My wanderings give me a good knowledge of the land (when I'm not too delirious or miserable to notice). I find Borderlander camps—not many, most discovered by the smell—and countryside lacking signs of human interference. I stick to these areas, though it's tempting to creep to the edge of the camps just to see another person.

I spent all my normal life surrounded by people and the last ten years living with my brother, crammed in an encampment with thousands of comrades. To suddenly be alone is a shocking black hole I ignore during the day and lose myself in at night.

By the end of May, I'm a wreck. Woozy, exhausted, talking to myself all the time. I can count my ribs and hang things from my hipbones. But I have to keep walking, even if it's more tortured zombie shuffle than graceful stroll.

If I stop, I may never get back up.

* * *

I lurch across a desolate moorland reflecting my state of mind, chewing on the last of my bitter and unsatisfying dandelion leaves. A patch of bright green blazes near the top of a hill and

10

I scramble towards it.

Blaeberries!

It doesn't matter that the other plants I passed were not in fruit. These ones will be.

I guess I'm an optimist after all.

My shaking fingers paw at the slender shrubs. Nothing but globular pink flowers. I scowl and kick at the heather. The branches capture my foot and I tumble into their springiness, huffing the smoked dirt smell of peat.

I close my eyes.

How easy it would be to die. How difficult it is to live.

"Get up, you bloody weakling," I say, my voice scratchy and gruff.

At the crest of the hill, the moorland stretches towards another, larger rise. Rusted wind turbines tower beyond it, their blades silent and still.

I should probably turn back, stick to the woodlands. This place is barren.

My boots shuffle up the incline. The wind swirls a stench of charred death. I blink to clear a grey haze from my eyeballs but it stays.

Not a haze—smoke.

"We've got a live one!" a voice cackles.

Icy adrenaline tingles to my fingertips and batters my heart against my ribs. I sway at the top of the hill, the burst of energy threatening to lead to faint rather than flight.

A huge Borderlander camp sprawls on the edge of the abandoned wind farm, the ramshackle collection of stone shelters and ragged tents clustered around an ancient Portakabin decorated with animal skins and skulls. Dirty faces gape at me, their owners clothed in a shabby collection of materials. Fires smoulder in front of several dwellings, dented pots steaming on crude tripods. The cooking food isn't enough to overcome the stink of unwashed bodies and human waste.

"Get him!" the same voice yells.

A gunshot cracks. I yelp and fall into the heather in a hail of tiny white flowers, bruising my spine on my worldly possessions. I roll to my feet and sprint down the hill, floundering between mounds of peat. A bellowing crowd pours over the rise, three men in front, one carrying what looks like a spear, the other two clutching rifles.

"Stop!" one says. "We only want to invite you to dinner."

"You'll be the main course," says another.

Cannibals. Great. What did I expect? A peaceful society who'd welcome me, feed me and present me with their most eligible women as a gift?

Would be nice, though.

I zoom past the patch of worthless blaeberry plants, my arms flapping to keep my balance on the uneven ground. The edge of a pot pounds my back. The three men pull ahead of the crowd. A straggling band has already halted, watching the chase from the base of the first hill.

My right foot hits nothing but air and I pitch forward. Stunted birch trees at the bottom of the short cliff rise up to greet me. I crunch through, my arms shielding my face. A sharp tug halts my descent. My boots dangle a metre from the ground, my sheet wedged between branches.

The yelling gets closer. A grimy face peeks over the cliff edge, his lank hair grease-stiffened and bald in places. He grins and aims his rifle. My bullet catches him in the throat and his gun clatters to the base of the crag.

My heels kick against bark. The sheet rips but doesn't loosen.

The other two men reach the cliff. I fire and they duck out of sight. I scrabble at the knot across my chest. The ends of the sheet slip free and my feet hit the ground, fronds of bracken slapping my face. My sheet stays lodged. I launch myself at it and yank. The sheet unravels, scattering my precious objects into the vegetation. I lose my grip and thud onto my back, my breath blasting out. I crawl to the nearest item and close my hand on a lighter. A bullet snaps through the branches and puffs into the dirt. The ground rumbles as the crowd catches up.

I run. Bullets whizz into the heather. I fire behind me without looking, darting for the conifer trees marking the end of the moorland. Down and down I gallop, reaching the bottom where the space becomes lighter, greener. I splash through a shallow river, desperately thirsty, and up a slight incline to a sun-dappled meadow.

The trees reel, a white haze blurring the leaves. A stitch sinks claws into my side and burrows for my spleen. I blink and find myself on my face, panting into the grass.

The next blink lasts a long time.

11

A butterfly saves my life.

The beautiful, fuzzy thing perches on a daisy in front of my nose, fluttering wings tipped orange and mottled green.

I pluck it from the flower and stuff it in my mouth.

Tastes like powdery cabbage.

I crawl to the edge of the meadow, ignoring the flying insects buzzing out of reach. It takes a ridiculous amount of heaving and grunting to flip a rotten log. Beetles and spiders scurry from the exposed cavity. I grab them and try not to think.

Crunch, crunch. Swallow.

My imagination provides the twitching legs scraping my throat on the way down.

A shaft of sunlight bathes a moving mound of pine needles and I scoop fistfuls of ants, licking my palms to get them all. A mouthful of wood sorrel chases the bitterness.

I'm almost full.

Just don't throw up. I don't want to see what my stomach contents look like with bits of carapace and hundreds of spindly legs—

I lurch to my feet and continue through the woods, not caring where I go. I gather snails and edible plants into a pouch made by my t-shirt. Plantain, dock, chickweed, pignuts. I chew on more sorrel to ease the unbearable thirst, tormenting myself by following the burble of a river. It weaves between slick rocks and tumbles in gorges of dripping ferns.

I can almost taste it. The cool freshness, crisp and clear and glorious.

I have to drink it. So what if I die? Dehydration will kill me as easily as any toxin.

The trees end, the river widening into a pool to form a secluded basin circled by the forest and bordered on two thirds by fine, white sand. Three deer lap water at the edge. They raise their heads and bound into the woods.

Deer. Drinking. Water. *Drinking water.*

I release my grip on my t-shirt, scattering snails and leaves, and stagger to the shimmering pool. I drop to my knees and shove my face under the surface, sucking water and mud and pieces of vegetation. The rush of cold soothes my throat and swirls into my belly. Water beads in my eyelashes, my hair stuck to my cheeks, t-shirt sodden. Half-drowned, I toss my lighter, knife and gun onto the beach and wriggle into the pool, gasping at the chill. I scrub myself with handfuls of sand, scouring my skin until it glows pink. A dirty scum floats on the surface, a month's worth of despair and struggle. I dive into the cool dark and swim out to the centre, coming up for air on a burst of laughter.

A small waterfall splashes into the pool opposite the beach, flanked by a rocky crag. Near where the river flows away, a sheltered dip holds pondweed and water lilies, the buds of flowers as large as my fist.

Shivering, I paddle out, water sloshing off my clothes and in my belly. I strip and squeeze the excess from my navy t-shirt and combats, propping my boots on a rock to dry. I strap my holster around my hips to be safe.

God, if people could see me now—naked, scrawny, my body covered in bruises and scrapes.

Starvation and anguish aren't sexy.

I collect wood and dried moss for kindling in the gloom of the surrounding forest. A hastily flung stone kills two pigeons. I roast them on my fire, giggling a little hysterically, their feathers stuck to my fingers.

Two birds, one stone. Get it?

I cook the snails too slow to slither to freedom in the embers of the fire. Once they stop bubbling, I hook them out on a sharpened twig and swallow them whole, burning my mouth. They smell and taste like chicken.

Freaking delicious.

Fed, hydrated and semi-clean, it's the happiest I've been for weeks.

If I ignore the dead brother and destroyed home.

I flop in the sand and doze as the day darkens to evening, my clothes steaming gently.

I imagine Dylan sprawled on the other side of the fire, chewing on a grass stalk. We talk about girls, it being his favourite topic of conversation. He could never understand how I got more women. He slagged me for being a skinny emo but I have muscles where it counts. And women go crazy for the messy black hair and violet eyes. Sometimes all I had to do was look at them…

"But Giselle only liked you. Explain that mystery." I prop myself on my elbow. "Dylan?"

The fire is out but the white sand glows in the darkness, showing a stretch of empty beach.

It takes me a second to remember, so convinced he'll be there, grinning and telling me to go fuck myself.

Fresh loss clenches my stomach. I hunch, my eyes prickling, and cuddle my knees to my chest.

"Don't you dare cry," I say but my voice wobbles, ruining the effect. "You've cried enough."

I shove to my feet and stalk to the edge of the woodland. I make my bed in the canopy and pretend to sleep.

* * *

The pool and surrounding forest provide an astonishing bounty.

I lash my knife to a branch with strips of bark and stab fish from the water. The aquatic vegetation attracts flies that taste like duck and the stems hold clusters of water boatman eggs.

Mmm, caviar.

Edible plants support a host of insects in the woods. I pick strawberries and tart little apples, munch on pignuts and sweet carrots dug from the soil. Chanterelles and bird eggs add more variety.

I put on weight, have more energy. Stop blundering around.

It's peaceful and quiet. Occasional explosions carry on the wind, too distant to worry about. I enjoy the isolation during the day. It keeps me safe.

But I can't trick myself at night.

Sleeping is the only time I relax my guard for short bursts. I manage a couple of hours, three at the most, before jerking awake, my heart tripping, breath held. I can't even escape into pleasant dreams. Nightmares of finding Dylan in the rubble, of being chased through trees, of screaming for help in the dark, plague me the second I shut my eyes.

Doubt and fear and misery multiply in the blackness. I have three bullets left. Three cylinders of metal until nothing stands between me and the next abomination longing to rip my throat out.

What's the point in delaying the inevitable? My situation isn't going to change. The war seems to be continuing indefinitely, the dragon either buried or gathering dust, the morons too stupid to control her. Do I really want this to be my life? Struggling for every morsel, surrounded by enemies.

Alone.

Two things stop me from committing suicide—the promise I made to Stig, and Dylan. If I die, there may be no one else around who remembers him. No one to keep his memory alive.

At least I don't believe in meeting him again in the afterlife or I probably would've topped myself ages ago.

12

The morning dawns beautiful and clear. I scowl at the sun warming the air and shimmering through the leaves.

I spent a restless night unable to get comfortable, crippled by loneliness and the yearning for human contact. A hug. Animal sex.

Is that too much to ask?

I scrape my arm sliding from my current sleeping tree and kick the trunk, bruising my toes.

"Fuck you," I snarl. "Fuck this. Fuck *everything*."

Dylan would be shocked. Who am I kidding? He'd be proud of my decaying vocabulary and encourage me to use swear words as adjectives, like a real man.

God, I wish he were here.

I stomp to my food cairn on the beach, munching leaves and berries and slurping raw eggs without tasting them.

Exercise. That's what I need. I'm outside but still cooped up. Maybe I can find some proper red meat. The blandness of fish and birds is damned boring.

I drink water from the pool and splash some on my face, chewing on a hazel twig to clean my teeth. I enter the trees at a brisk pace, head down, arms swinging, barrelling through the undergrowth. The woods end and I barely slow. Fields, scrub. Fields, scrub. More trees.

All the bloody same.

Intent on frowning at the ground, I almost walk into a small Borderlander camp. I suck in a breath and dive behind a pile of rocks.

No cries of alarm or excited yells about cooking me drift to my hiding place.

Animal skin lean-to's huddle around the remains of a country estate. A grubby baby crawls out of a tent, half its tiny face scarred. It gurgles amidst the detritus and disappears through a doorway.

I trot away from the camp, my hand on my gun. "Pay attention, you jackass."

To make up for my carelessness, I prowl through the forest, my eyes scanning, shoulders tense. Each cautious step avoids snapping branches. Leaves rustle to my left. I freeze.

Please be a deer. Or a sheep. I'll even take a rabbit.

My stomach rumbles. I draw my Browning and part the bushes, expecting the flash of a fluffy white tail.

Soulless black eyes meet mine.

I scramble backwards. The lynx vaults the shrubbery, its barking growl tightening my balls and shivering through my chest. It looks almost natural with its tufted ears and spotted, tawny fur. A layer of flesh covers the armoured skeleton.

"Nice kitty," I murmur, edging away. "There's a good kitty."

Another growl rumbles from its throat. The muscles in its legs bunch. I fire without thinking. The bullet thuds into the beast's shoulder. It screams and springs at me. My boots fly across the ground. Heavy paws thump in pursuit.

Too fast. It's too fast.

I roll, and metal claws tug at my t-shirt. The lynx shrieks, twisting in mid-air to follow me. I clap my hand to my side.

No blood.

Keep running.

The trees dwindle to scrub and waist-high grass. My boot connects with a root, slamming me to the ground. The lynx roars in triumph. I flip onto my back and squeeze the trigger. The bullet clangs into the lynx's skull. It shakes its head and hisses, flashing fangs. I clamp both hands around my gun to keep it steady. My finger tightens. The lynx lowers its head, its lips drawn back. I fire. The big cat jerks, legs thrashing, and flops sideways. One black orb glares at me, the other shattered where my bullet passed through into its cybernetic brain.

The only weak spot.

I collapse into the grass and stare at the sky, struggling to breathe past my heartbeat. A bee drones overhead, the sun warm. Late afternoon by its position. Miles from my secluded pool.

I won't make it back before dark.

And who cares? It's an illusion of paradise. It isn't safe. It isn't peaceful. Any abomination or soldier or insane Borderlander could discover it by accident and gut me.

I hold the Browning in front of my face.

Useless hunk of metal.

My fingers stiffen, my knuckles white. I want to toss it but can't seem to let go. Huffing, I sit up and holster it.

Maybe the threat will be enough.

For people, anyway.

My eyes dart over the grass. The stalks sway in the wind. A fly lands on the glistening corner of the lynx's mouth and scuttles inside, buzzing happily.

I can't even eat it. The skin is organic but the muscles are biomechanical, composed of nanofibrils.

Mmm, fibrils.

I aim a kick at its thick skull on my way past and scavenge a quick meal—mostly invertebrate-based—before climbing a tree. The sun sets in a blaze of orange and gold.

I try not to think about dying.

How long will I last with only a knife? A couple of days? A week? My death won't be pretty. Maybe a hunting party of Borderlanders will chuck me in a pot and make a Blake stew. Or another abomination will corner me, its claws slicing bloody furrows, its muzzle buried in my abdomen.

Better to end it myself. Quick, clean. Cut my wrists and drift away. I had a good run. What was it, two months?

I count on my fingers.

It's the 22nd of June.

"Are you kidding me?" I sigh, leaning my head on the rough trunk and shutting my eyes. "Well, a happy freaking birthday to me."

13

My mood fails to improve the next day. A depressive lethargy traps me in the tree, slumped and breathing, one finger tracing endless circles on the bark. The sun bakes the canopy and trickles sweat down my face. Thirst and images of dunking myself in my cool, clear pool force me to move.

I walk deeper into the forest, a hand on my gun out of habit. A small burn burbles down a rocky slope, a blackbird bathing in the shallows, scattering droplets that twinkle in the dappled sunlight. It arrows away into the trees instead of keeling over.

I drink from my cupped palms and splash my face, pressing cold fingers to the back of my neck.

It's time to go. It'll still be getting dark when I get back to my pool, if I hurry.

At least I'll die somewhere picturesque.

I head away from the burn but freeze before I can take more than two steps.

What the hell am I *doing?* I can't wander around anymore. I have no bullets. I'm a picnic for anything with teeth.

I scramble up the nearest tree and curl into a ball. A horrible nausea grips my stomach.

It's too dangerous to move. Too dangerous to stay. Too dangerous to live.

I press my forehead to my knees and struggle to get myself under control.

This is no place for a panic attack. Just breathe. In, out, in, out. Repeat. Everything will be fine.

Yeah, right. From optimistic to downright delusional.

My heart rate slows. I call myself a few names for motivation and slither onto my belly, lowering my foot to the next branch.

An explosion vibrates in my palms gripping the tree. Crows burst from the canopy and scatter into the sky.

What now? Why did I leave my nice little pool?

What a bloody idiot.

Smoke blooms directly ahead, the source far enough to be cloaked by vegetation. Someone screams. I climb higher, tucking myself against the trunk. The screams fade as if the person is being carried away rather than dying.

Although, from the sounds of it, dying is a possibility.

I hold my breath, my eyes scanning the gaps in the leaves. A twig snaps. Movement flickers between the trees and a woman stumbles into view. A wild tumble of blonde hair. Breasts.

For god's sake, of course she has breasts. It's only been two months, you animal.

She's wearing a t-shirt and combats, a huge green rucksack with black zips on her shoulders. A slim, grey contraption is strapped to her left arm, a Glock 17 at her waist.

Not a Borderlander.

She trips and falls down a slope, thrusting to her feet and flinging the rucksack off. Muttering to herself, she paces in a circle, her path taking her under my hiding place.

The rucksack will have everything I need to survive. She's obviously doing fine out here. Clean, smooth skin, barely a scratch on her. Ask her for help? Sure. She'll shoot me in the face.

This is no place for social niceties.

I shift position, easing further out from the trunk, my boots balanced on a branch. Leaves rustle. The woman tenses, starts to turn. I drop onto her back and slam her to the ground. Her breath rushes out. I press my gun to her head and a knee to her spine.

If she fights, she'll soon realise I have no bullets.

I yank the Glock from her holster and switch it with my gun, tucking the Browning into my waistband.

Hello, sweet bullets.

I jerk the other weapon off her arm and toss it aside for later.

"Where are you from?" I say, adrenaline and relief harshening the words. "What are you doing here?"

A furious, jade-green eye glares at me through a tangle of hair.

The stuff falls almost to her waist; I'm practically sitting on it. How does it not annoy the crap out of her?

Why am I thinking about her hair?

She says nothing.

Ah, the silent treatment. Misguided weapon of woman-kind.

I hook her dog-tags out the back of her t-shirt.

Two pairs, like me, but hers have the same name. Carmichael. It seems familiar. Different factions—Soldiers of the Lost and…

My hand clenches, metal scraping together and digging into my palm.

"Why two? Which one are you from?"

"Neither," she says in a soft, haughty voice. "I'm starting a collection."

I rap her on the head with the butt of the Glock.

"Ow! For fuck's sake, I'm from Calders. They were destroyed, so I went to Fellhill."

Rage scorches my stomach and boils up my throat. "You're The People's Republic?"

She's the reason I'm here. Lost, alone, aching. Her goddamn faction.

I tug my dog-tags free—my ones, not Dylan's—and shove them in her face. She squints but her reaction is unmistakable. She flinches, the one eye I can see flying to mine.

"Your faction destroyed my home," I snarl.

"I had nothing to do with it"—her eye narrows—"though you goddamn deserved it."

My fingers itch to wrap around her throat. "How would you know what we deserved? You don't know the first thing about us."

"You abused the poor woman. What did you expect her to do, leave you untouched?"

"No," I spit, air whistling through my nose.

But she should've been satisfied with killing Wick and destroying the torture chamber. That was retribution. The rest of us did nothing to her. What right did she have to slaughter us all?

"Then what are you pissed about? You would've done the same in her position."

How dare she lie here and act the victim?

"She's—the reason—my brother—is dead."

The woman stills as if gathering herself.

Go on, bitch, gloat. See where it gets you.

"I—I'm sorry. Losing family—is worse than anything."

I almost batter her with the gun again before the words penetrate. A lump stoppers my throat, grief dulling the anger.

My eyes prickle and I look away, loath to show her any weakness.

"I don't need your pity."

"It's not pity."

"Whatever. I don't need it." I frown at the trees, the gun steady on her head. "What happened to her?"

"She died. When Fellhill attacked Calders."

As I suspected. I may have gotten some closure killing her myself but dead is dead. Dylan can punish her in the imaginary afterlife of my dreams.

"Why did they take you in?" I say.

"Maybe I impressed them."

"Then what're you doing way down here?"

"None of your damn business."

Excellent. I prefer the attitude to her fake sympathy. She seems a fine surrogate for atonement.

"And there we were, getting all friendly," I say. "Stand up."

I shove to my feet and step out of reach, scooping the long contraption from the ground. Clamping it between my left arm and my ribs, I quickly fasten the straps.

The woman rolls onto one elbow. "Why?"

"Because I'll shoot you if you don't."

She stands slowly, her arms at her sides. I point her Glock at her head.

Red flares on high cheekbones. "Your gun's empty, isn't it?"

"Yup."

"You arrogant son-of-a-bitch."

Arrogant, who me? Crazy lucky more like.

"I'm surprised that mouth hasn't got you killed."

"There's still time."

Huh. Blonde but not unintelligent.

I flick the barrel of her Glock. "Put your hands on that tree and spread your legs."

"Why?"

God, she's annoying.

"Would you just bloody do it?"

Pouting, she stomps to the tree and slaps her palms on the trunk, though her legs are barely an inch apart. I kick her foot and she widens her stance.

"Don't move."

"Yes, boss."

"Seriously, how are you not dead?"

How did Marshall put up with her insubordination? Maybe she was one of his whores. She's pretty enough. Perhaps she put her mouth to other uses.

Must not think about her mouth.

Keeping the gun in one hand, I slide my fingers through her hair. She flinches but doesn't resist. I circle the collar of her t-shirt and pat her back. She hunches her shoulders and I roll my eyes.

Christ, you'd think I was fondling her. Or maybe she resents being touched by someone as filthy as me.

Snobbish and mouthy—every man's dream.

I run my hands over the rest of her. Curvy, decent tits, firm arse.

Would you stop it.

I remove a small, unknown handgun model and a knife from her boot. No other weapons. I ditch my tattered holster and fasten hers around my waist.

It's time to get this done and return to my pool. Find out what goodies I've won.

I wave vaguely in the direction of a lighter space in the trees, the shadows lengthening between the trunks. "Walk."

She stalks into the undergrowth, her face sullen. I hoist the rucksack onto my shoulders.

The damn thing is heavy.

The woman whirls around, her eyes flashing.

Oh, she does *not* like me having the rucksack. I bet she won't survive without it.

Pampered, this one.

"Stop," I say. "Sit against the tree."

She halts near the edge of the clearing, sliding down the trunk of a birch and sitting in the dirt. She drops her eyes.

It's a bit late for the demure act.

"Put your arms behind you, around the trunk."

She hesitates. "I'm sorry someone from Calders destroyed Livingston but what else do you want me to say?"

"There's nothing you can say."

Nothing she says, nothing she does, will bring Dylan back. All I can hope for is a sliver of satisfaction, knowing someone shares my misery.

May as well be her.

I walk behind the tree, shrugging off the rucksack, my movements hurried in case she decides to do something dumb.

Part of me wants her to fight. Shooting her might release some of the anger slicing my insides.

I pull a braided rope from a side pocket and bind her wrists, avoiding a bandage on her left forearm.

Okay, so maybe she has one scratch on her.

She wriggles under my hands but doesn't try to escape.

"What happened to your arm?" I stop at her feet, the Glock hanging at my side.

"I'll tell you if you untie me."

"I don't think so."

"Then don't bother to fucking ask if you're going to leave me to die." Fury darkens her eyes to emerald.

I guess she has a point. What does it matter anyway?

I pull her flick knife from my pocket and toss it. "If you cut yourself loose, maybe you'll survive out here. If not… It's more of a chance than my brother had."

"I didn't do anything! Are you not goddamn listening?"

Funny how the people who didn't do anything get hurt the worst.

I turn and walk away before she makes me feel something ridiculous, like guilt.

"Wait!"

"You might have enough time to get free before dark. I'd start now."

"You purple-eyed bastard! It's a war, people die."

Purple-eyed bastard? That's rich coming from a green-eyed harpy.

I pause at the edge of the clearing. "You're right, people die."

She struggles against the rope. I shuffle through the undergrowth to drown out her panicked gasps.

"What was she supposed to do?" she yells, her breath hitching. "What the hell would you have done? Answer me that—what the fuck would you have done any different?"

My smile is brittle. "Absolutely nothing."

14

I don't go far despite my new weapons. Only far enough so it won't be easy to find me if she cuts herself free quickly.

She should be grateful I didn't shoot her. We're enemies, even minus the dead brother and destroyed faction. Although, knowing how short and miserable her life will be out here, killing her may have been a mercy.

But I am not going to feel guilty. I spent most of the damn war feeling guilty while others suffered under Wick's hands and look where it got me.

Attracted by the gurgle of water, I follow a river into a narrow gorge of deepening shadows. The sides widen at a bend, a shallow cave scooped from the rock. I unpack the rucksack, astonished by the contents: water quality monitor, food, bedding, cooking utensils and heat blocks, first aid kit, clothes, a control pad and a heavy object the size and shape of a potato. I turn it over in my fingers, the surface smooth and cool. Puzzled, I set it aside, more excited by the prospect of a proper wash.

The river tests clean. I strip and jump in, hissing at the cold. It takes two soap capsules smelling of almonds and honey to make me human again. I scrub my clothes, filthy bubbles swirling downstream, and climb out. I palm the water off and dry with a microfiber towel no bigger than my hand. A dark green t-shirt and combats are snug across my shoulders and thighs but not bad.

The woman and I must be the same size.

Dylan would piss himself at that.

No boxer shorts, though, and I'm not desperate enough to wear women's underwear.

I fill a water bottle and bend to pick up the heavy potato thing, my bare foot kicking the control pad. I open the opaque protective lid covering four coloured buttons. I press green and the metal potato vanishes.

What in the hell…

I peer at the spot where it was. The moist rock ripples. I pass my hand over it, my fingers brushing a cool, smooth surface.

A cloaking device! Wow. But why does something so small need to be hidden?

The potato reappears on another push of the green button. Red and black do nothing. I thumb the blue button and the thing expands to chest height, sending me backwards, close to toppling in the river.

A sleeping pod! No more freaking trees.

A laser security system in a black dome sits on the flattened roof.

A safe place to sleep. A refuge.

This is more than I could've hoped for.

No wonder the woman didn't want me to take the rucksack.

My finger hovers over the red button.

Will it activate the security system?

I brace myself and press black. A round portal slides open to a pearlescent interior. I toss everything inside and dive in, the floor spongy under my knees. Two more pushes of the black button seal and lock the portal with a thud. The sound of the river still burbles through the solid walls alongside the lazy song of birds settling for the night. I press the red switch, pretty confident it triggers the security system. The green button renders me invisible.

The woman will never find me but she knows that. I imagine her despair, the frustration and hate.

Now we have things in common.

I stuff myself with boil-in-the-bag curry, close to tears when I discover instant coffee, sugar and dried milk among the bounty.

God, it's been years!

Wick would've banned it, if we had any. It's too close to happiness for his liking.

I inhale fragrant steam, a grin stretching my face.

This is how to survive no man's land. Sure, the coffee and food won't last but I can feed myself. Forage and hunt. Whatever the grey weapon is, it's rechargeable going by the solar panels.

My ammo will never run out.

I inflate a pillow and wriggle into the sleeping bag. Warm and comfortable and safe. I fall asleep immediately but, despite my sudden good fortune, my dreams aren't peaceful. Replays of Wick's torture videos dog me through the night. The screams, the moist ripping of flesh. The begging. On and on to the last. The one woman who fought and escaped. Pretty face, dark hair. No, not dark, wet. Blonde? Defiant green eyes. And her voice, fear-husky but still soft. Still distinctive.

I snap awake. "You lying little bitch."

It was *her*. The one who obliterated my encampment and murdered my brother. I had her right there, in my hands, and she tricked me.

I scrabble out of the sleeping bag and stuff objects blindly into the rucksack, cursing the woman with every horrible name I can think of.

The opal light is bright.

Does that mean it's daylight outside? Am I too late?

No. I found her once, I'll find her again. She is not getting away. She has to pay.

I tumble out of the portal, reducing the pod and nearly trapping my foot in the shrinking doorway. Late morning sunlight bathes my face. I growl at it, throwing the rucksack on and sprinting back the way I came.

I skid to a panting halt. "*Think*. Don't be a jackass. She must know you'd remember. And rush into her trap."

Bitch. The manipulative, hateful, murdering bitch.

I tear through the woods in the opposite direction, bursting into the meadow where the lynx tried to eat me. The rubble of a farmhouse juts out of the grass. I hide the rucksack under a rusted sheet of corrugated metal and gallop into the forest, straight for the clearing. Nearing it, I force myself to slow and catch my breath.

I need to be calm. Coldly professional. Not let her see she's rattled me.

I circle the clearing, my careful steps hushed. The body of an abomination lies in the centre, some kind of boar/wolf splice.

No sign of the woman.

A frustrated howl builds in my throat. I creep into the clearing, scanning for signs of the route she's taken. Branches snap. A shape drops from a tree and thumps into the grass.

"Mother-*fucker*," growls the foliage.

She has no idea I'm here. Man, she's in for a shock.

Morning, sweetheart.

"You really have a mouth on you." My thudding heartbeat trembles in my voice but she probably won't notice.

Silence.

She sits up, her eyes wide, clutching her right arm to her chest. A swirl of emotions runs across her face, too fast to read.

As long as one is crap-your-pants fear, I don't care about the rest.

She rises to her knees. "Sorry if it offends your delicate sensibilities but I can't say 'darn it' when a good 'fuck' will do."

My mouth gapes.

She's making fricking *jokes?* Does she have no clue how close she is to death? It would be a kindness to kill her now. She deserves to suffer. To experience my pain crammed into a few terrible days.

She wobbles to her feet, sliding slender fingers towards her pocket.

I raise the contraption strapped to my left arm. "Take the knife out and toss it over here. If I see a hint of blade, I'll shoot you. This thing is on the highest setting."

"That *thing* is an electrigun," she says in her snooty voice.

"Great. I will electrocute your arse if you try to pin that knife in me."

She glowers and lobs the knife, inching towards me. It hits my chest but I force myself to stand still. I crouch, my eyes locked on hers, and scoop the knife from the ground. She swallows.

Finally. A hint of unease.

"You back to finish me off?" she says. "What happened to giving me a chance?"

"You lied to me."

Her face pales. "I don't know what you're talking about."

"I know who you are. Wick showed us video of you in the torture chamber. You're the one who destroyed my encampment and murdered my brother. Not so clever, are you?"

She reels as if I've hit her and sags against a tree. Her eyes look huge, the colour gone from her cheeks.

I can read her expression now—horror and shame.

"You saw—what he did?"

She sways. I take a step without realising, as if I might... What? Give her a freaking hug?

Don't you dare feel sorry for her!

"Only your arrival," I huff, embarrassed by my reaction. Goddamn bleeding heart. "Jesus, woman, take a breath."

She slumps to her knees and pants into the grass. "Fuck. *You.*"

It lacks her usual heat.

What does she think I saw?

"What did Wick do to you?"

She drags herself upright with the aid of the tree. I can see her legs quivering from here.

Dammit, a wounded deer routine isn't what I want. I want defiance. Shrieking. For her to call me a bastard and gloat about my brother's death so I can punch her face in.

"As if you don't know. You lived with him. Did you all watch his videos like a—like a goddamn movie?" She hunches around herself, her fingers rubbing her chest as though it aches.

The gesture is familiar. I fist my hand to stop from copying it.

Who knew I was such an empath?

"He forced us. Most of us. There was no choice."

She drops her gaze. "No choice but to survive as best you could."

Is that what she thinks she's done? Obliterated Livingston so she could survive? What happened with Wick? Does she believe she was justified? That he drove her to it?

It doesn't matter. Okay, it was probably agonising and traumatic. But she didn't have to punish the rest of us.

Living with Wick was punishment enough.

I open my mouth to tell her to quit the sad-eyed performance.

"I'm sorry," I say.

Well, crap.

She blinks her lovely eyes at me.

"I'm sorry you were tortured," I continue.

Would you shut up! She doesn't deserve absolution.

Or does she? Just as she knows nothing about me, I know nothing about what she suffered under Wick.

Almost nothing. I saw the other videos. Have been in there myself.

"Can we stop talking about it, please?" she whispers.

God, I have no idea what I'm doing.

I nod, one hand resting on the Glock at my waist. "Start walking that way."

She opens her mouth.

"Nope. No questions about why or where or any sassy comments."

She shoves away from the tree, the colour returning to her face. "Just one question. No sass."

"Woman, do you never give up?"

"It's one of my best qualities. And my name is Anita, not woman."

I laugh.

Dammit. How did she do that?

I school my face into a frown. "Fine, *Anita*, one question."

"Are you going to kill me?"

Yes. No. I don't bloody know.

Why is this confusing? She killed Dylan. She deserves to die. That's all there is to it.

But…

I need to think. More information. Maybe she's a nice person—*as if that matters*—and destroying Livingston is the wickedest thing she's done. Maybe she regrets it.

And would I have done the same?

I sigh. "Not right now."

"Comforting," she says.

I snort.

Great. I'm stuck with a comedian.

"Question answered. Walk."

I shake my head and follow her into the trees.

What would Dylan think of me, sparing his killer—disgusted, proud of my benevolence? Glad I found someone to talk to?

At least I know what he'd be doing if he were here.

Flirting desperately and trying to hump her.

15

With no other place to go, I take her to my pool, forcing her to carry the rucksack in the hope it will tire her out. Stop her mouthing off.

Though that may make the decision on whether to kill her or not easier.

She expands the pod on the sand, facing the portal towards the waterfall.

Of course a woman would think about waking up to a pretty view.

I perch on a rock and watch her. Sweat darkens her t-shirt and moulds it to her back.

She's slim but muscled, like me.

I guess she didn't just sit on her arse and let others do the hard work.

She tosses the sleeping gear inside the pod and crouches next to the rucksack. Her eyes flick to me.

I point the electrigun. "Take your hand out of the bag."

She straightens, her palms out. No threat here.

Yeah, right. She was going for the control pad. Jump through the portal, press the red button.

Goodbye, Blake.

"Get in the pod," I say.

"Can I wash first?"

I smirk. "Be my guest."

She bends for the rucksack, her hair falling over her shoulder.

"Nice try. Back up."

She raises her hands and retreats. I grab the control pad.

It's dangerous to underestimate her cunning.

I hand her a soap capsule. "The water's safe. I've drunk it before."

I return to the rock and flop in the sand, the electrigun balanced on my knee.

"You're going to watch me?" she says with a curl of her lip.

"You clearly can't be trusted, so yes. Keep your clothes on if it makes you feel better."

"How generous."

I obviously haven't tired her out enough.

She kicks off her boots, padding into the pool in her socks. The water creeps up her long legs. Chest-deep, she breaks the soap capsule over her head and massages it down her body. I drag my eyes away to scan the tree line.

She sloshes out and I can't resist looking.

To make sure she's behaving, of course.

Her clothes hug the curve of thigh, breast and hip, her flat belly. Wet hair clings to her shoulders and back.

It's similar to how she arrived in the torture chamber.

"That's why I didn't recognise you immediately," I say. "You looked like this—darker hair, wet."

She sticks her nose in the air and stalks into the pod, trailing drips.

I scowl at my boots. "Why don't you just tell her every stupid thing that pops into your head?"

Less babbling moron, more terrifying captor.

After two minutes, I walk to the pod. Anita is sitting in a pair of green combats and my navy t-shirt.

"Wearing my clothes already?"

She crosses her arms, though she blushes. "You're wearing my clothes."

Can't argue with that.

I toss the rucksack inside, spreading her sodden clothes on the rocks to dry. I duck into the pod and lock the portal. Anita scoots to the back, her arms wrapped around her legs.

Well, this is awkward. How does one converse with one's captive? I've never taken a prisoner before.

Christ, man, you don't need to talk to her or keep her entertained. You can do whatever you want.

I pull another coil of rope from the rucksack. "Hold out your hands."

"I need to change my bandage."

Fine, delay the inevitable.

I pass her the bag of dressing materials. She unravels the sopping bandage to expose a long laceration on her forearm.

A knife wound. Sharp blade. Few days old.

"What happened? I actually wanted to know."

Why do I care? No idea. Maybe her pain soothes my own.

She frowns at her arm, her slim fingers re-bandaging the injury. "John Anders tried to gut me."

How did she tangle with him so recently? She would have met him in Lowkirk when she was a prisoner. Before Wick captured her. Maybe she ran into him still picking over the wreckage of Livingston. Or Calders.

He's a bit of a vulture.

Did she kill him? John doesn't tend to stop once he gets stabbing.

I wait but the stubborn set of her mouth tells me no more details will be forthcoming.

I sigh. "Hold out your hands, wrists together."

She doesn't move. Her eyes glint at me.

"Are you going to make me do this the hard way?"

She bares her teeth. "Probably."

I lunge but she bats my hand away and aims a punch at my face. I grab her wrist and yank her across my leg, pinning her arms behind her back. She wriggles, her warm breasts pressing into my thigh.

"You're getting tied up, Anita. Your choice is whether your hands are behind you—which will hurt more—or in front. Keep struggling and I'll truss you up so tight, you won't be able to move."

"Goddamn you," she pants.

That's right, baby. May as well surrender.

She jerks one arm free and shoves herself up.

Man, she's strong.

I roll on top of her, sitting on her shoulder blades and pressing her arms flat to the floor above her head.

"This is really not endearing you to me."

"*Good*," she snarls.

"You might want to reconsider since I'm the one deciding if you deserve to live."

I bind her wrists, keeping my full weight on her. She doesn't curse me so she probably can't breathe. I spin and straddle her arse, sliding my hands down her legs.

"You don't have to do this. We've both lost someone to the war."

I hunch, picturing the white face and blue-tinged lips. The awful grating of bones in his crushed chest.

"Yes, but I didn't kill your sister," I say.

Carmichael. I recognised the surname from her dog-tags before The People's Republic part distracted me.

And everyone knew Ailsa.

"That's not fair," Anita says. "You have *no* idea… You can't just—"

No idea—is she kidding? I lived with Wick and saw what he could do. Had a taste of it myself. Dylan was the only thing that kept me sane, the only bright spot in a world darker by the day. And she ripped him from me, snuffing out his life as if it were nothing.

I tie her ankles and crawl off, struggling to control the loss hollowing my stomach.

I am not freaking crying in front of her, no way.

I bow my head and glare at my fists, inhaling scorching air. She squirms into a sitting position. I meet her gaze and she flinches.

"That's not fair." She tugs at the ropes, all elbows and knees. Her breathing speeds. "I had to do… I had no… I had to. I *had* to."

Her voice rises, her face pale apart from two pink spots on her cheeks. She contorts her wrists, her fingers scrabbling for the knots. Her ribs heave, sucking whoops of air. The skin around her wrists and ankles blooms red.

"Anita, you're going to hurt yourself. Anita?"

She twists her wrists and pulls at the bonds, her hands white, her eyes wild.

Christ, she's having a panic attack.

I shove her head down. "Breathe, Anita. Just breathe."

She trembles under my touch, the ridge of her spine beneath my palm, but the awful gasping slows.

I guess she doesn't like being tied up.

Of course she doesn't, you jackass. Who tied her up? Wick. Trapped and vulnerable and unable to fight. She had to lie there and endure whatever brought the horror and shame into her eyes at the thought of me witnessing it.

I remove my tingling hand instead of rubbing it up and down her warm back.

We need a distraction.

"What happened to the dragon?" I say.

Her head comes up. She meets my gaze, her face flushed, hair tousled. A spark of defiance. Embarrassed but powering through.

Thata girl.

"When she didn't bring the country to its knees, I figured something must've gone wrong," I say when she doesn't answer.

Her eyes search my face. I don't know if she finds what she's looking for but she straightens her spine.

"She was destroyed. A woman set fire to her interior while she was in Fellhill."

It's another spear of pain. Another loss. How much can one guy take?

"Deliberately?" I say, my voice husky.

She nods. "The woman was trying to frame me."

"She was jealous."

Why do women despise other women? Suzanne would have *hated* her. And because she's blonde. Rachael was blonde—a darker blonde, petite—but Suzanne wrote her off due to her scarred hands. A cooking accident in the kitchens. Personally, I was intrigued by how the roughness would feel sliding down—

Is this really the time?

"Easy guess," Anita says.

I shrug, glad she can't read my mind. "I have eyeballs."

"What—"

"Nothing. How did the dragon come to be in Fellhill? How were The People's Republic destroyed if they had her first?"

Anita's usual stubborn expression tightens her face.

I fight not to roll my eyes. "I just want to understand what happened to her. I helped build her."

"You built her? That's… She was… Amazing."

Ouch. She doesn't need to sound shocked.

"Don't let these looks fool you." I flip my hair off my forehead, treating her to a tiny dose of the moves that have dropped many a woman's pants.

She swallows, her eyes falling to her lap, her fingers playing with the rope.

Nervous? I still got it.

Would you quit teasing her.

"I wasn't in Calders when Fellhill attacked, neither was the dragon."

My humour evaporates. "So you lied again?"

"Simplified," she says with a scowl. "I was sent to Fellhill and they captured me, had me steal her from Calders. Then they made me one of them."

How many factions have taken her prisoner? Revolutionary Front, us and Soldiers of the Lost. How is she alive? And when did she go to Fellhill? There were only two weeks between her destroying Livingston and Calders being annihilated. She must have barely been injured if she managed to go on a damn assignment into the most fanatical faction of the lot of us. And why did Marshall let her risk herself?

I need freaking answers. Who the hell is this woman? Is everything she says a lie or half-truth?

I open my mouth but she raises her hands and cuts me off. "Is this so I don't throttle you in your sleep?"

Changing the subject—classic diversion. I could force her to talk but don't want to trigger another panic attack quite yet.

Maybe tomorrow.

I swallow the questions burning my throat. "Pretty much."

"You realise I could wrap my arm around your neck and squeeze with my elbow?"

I narrow my eyes.

Always with the lip.

"Okay, okay, I promise not to," she says. "Don't tie me up more."

"You are exhausting."

I turn away, my mind whirling, and prepare the bed to steady myself.

This is not going as I imagined it. Anita swings between defiance and a disarming vulnerability. No fear. Regret? Maybe. Annoying? Oh, massively.

She wriggles into the bed beside me, separated by a respectable arm's length. I lie on my back and listen to her breathe, the opal light darkening as the sun sets. The covers twitch, tented over her knees.

"I can feel that, you know."

She stops picking at the rope connecting her ankles. "Did you do some fancy knot-tying course? How to ensnare one's prisoner to prevent midnight throttling?"

I sigh. "Goodnight, Anita."

"Goodnight, Blake," she smirks.

That mouth is going to get her in trouble.

16

Anita immediately falls asleep, and isn't that another blow to the ego? I want her repentant, begging for forgiveness, not slumbering peacefully beside me as if I'm no threat at all.

I shove up on my elbow, ready to shake her awake and yell at her. She lies on her back, her head turned away. The dying light of the pod tints her cheek and parted lips. No sign of the mouthy pain in the arse that will be there when she opens her eyes and pouts at me. The chains of her two dog-tags curl against the soft beat of her pulse.

Why is she out here? Why did she leave the security of Fellhill? They're formidable even without the dragon.

I flop down and frown at the ceiling.

She'll probably never tell me but what can I do, torture her to make her talk?

I shudder and close my eyes, willing myself to fall asleep.

What a tiring day. It's strange having another person next to me after two months of loneliness but it's not restful.

I roll onto my side and get a faceful of hair. Almonds and cut grass. I inch closer. Not touching but near enough to feel her heat beneath the covers. I pretend she's someone I like and slip into sleep.

* * *

Furtive shifting wakes me.

What is she doing?

I open my eyes. Anita is sitting next to me, her legs tucked under her, her focus darting from where I stashed the weapons.

"Um, morning?" she says.

I smirk.

Caught.

She scoots away and I strap the weapons on.

"So how exactly will you decide if I *deserve* to live? A point-scoring system? Toss a coin?"

Friendly greeting straight to combative. Excellent. Nothing like a good fight to get the blood flowing.

I cock my eyebrow. "You could placate me rather than antagonise."

"Placate you? *Endear* myself to you?" She hugs her bound arms to her chest, her fists clenched. "And how exactly does one do that—lie back and think of goddamn England?"

My heart thumps. "Jesus Christ, woman, I'm not going to rape you."

"Damn straight you're not. You touch me and I'll kill you."

I have to admire her bravado despite wanting to slap her for daring to suggest I'd… I'm not some depraved psychopath. I don't need to resort to rape and murder to get my rocks off.

I shouldn't be surprised. Of course she thinks that. Tied up in the middle of nowhere. Too lovely for any man to possibly resist touching her. Sure. To be honest, I expected her to come on to me. To manipulate her freedom with the promise of her body…

Then I remember how Wick liked to ruin beautiful things.

I swallow. "Did Wick…"

Panic returns to her eyes. She sways and her throat bobs.

"You have no right to ask," she wheezes.

Oh, god. He did. He raped her. That horrible long body of his, panting his rotten breath in her face.

My stomach clenches. I can't stop the rush of pity.

What must it have felt like pinned beneath him, to have him force—

"Don't look at me like that," Anita snaps, and I jump. "He didn't. He tried, but he didn't."

The tightness in my gut eases. She glares at me but it's a fragile shield, the pain shimmering in her eyes.

Dammit. It's hard to hate her when she seems about to cry. Wounded and vulnerable. I suck at this vengeance crap. Or maybe it's because she's a woman. If she were a guy, she'd be dead already.

Who knew I was sexist?

I hold up my hands. "Okay, well I won't, either. Won't even try."

Her perplexed expression is worth the joke.

I untie her and we move outside. An awkward truce carries us through most of the day. She does everything I say without complaint: drags logs onto the beach to sit on, sets snares (hers are better than mine), gathers food. She doesn't even mouth off when I tell her to sew my ripped combats.

She sits with her back against the log opposite me, a needle flashing in the sunlight, warm wind stirring her hair. She pauses every two stitches and scans the trees, her hand twitching towards her waist.

"I've been here before, remember?" I say, unable to take it anymore. "It's as safe as anywhere can be."

Her screw-you eyes meet mine. "Long way from Livingston."

"Had the time. I travelled."

Oh, sure, *travelled*.

"How the hell"—she clears her throat—"did you… How are you not…"

"How the hell am I not dead?"

"Well, yeah."

Dumb glorious luck.

"Stayed in our bunker the first few days," I say, without the 'practically comatose' part, "but John Anders found it and buried it. I was the only one outside at the time. Scavenged what I could. Moved around."

No need to tell her I cried a lot.

"Slept in trees, drank only water animals drank from," I continue, omitting my diet of bugs. "You can survive on surprisingly little when you want to live."

"How many people were in the bunker?" she says in a hesitant voice quite unlike her usual haughty tone.

Is she wondering how many she slaughtered?

"A hundred or so. You used the dragon with chilling efficiency." She gulps but I go on. "We sent a runner to get help. That's when we found out Revolutionary Front had razed the rest of our encampments. The mood—hardly great to begin with—was pretty dismal after that."

"Was Stig there?"

I frown. "How do you know Stig?"

"He, ah, helped me." She hunches over my combats, sealing the rip in the knee with another couple of neat stitches and tying off the thread.

That's it? That's all she's going to say?

"You have to give me more than that," I growl.

She flinches. "Stig knocked Wick unconscious before… When Wick tried to rape me. He gave me a uniform and a gun. Told me where to go."

It explains his sudden interest in my wellbeing. Stig freed the prisoner and she killed us. She murdered Dylan because Stig finally listened to his conscience.

Unbelievable.

"And Wick? Did you kill him?"

She twitches at the name, my combats fisted in her hand.

"Yes," she whispers.

She certainly did a number on his face. It takes a lot of rage to batter someone to death.

I should know, I'm getting close to it.

"Stig was a friend of my brother, his *best* friend," I say so she can understand the betrayal.

Her head snaps up. "He said the dragon was the only way to escape."

"Did he know what you planned?"

"He told me not to kill everyone."

And she spared a hundred. How merciful.

"Well, he committed suicide three days after you obliterated us. Guess he couldn't live with the guilt."

But here you are, skipping around, the slaughterer of thousands.

Her throat works, her face pale. "I'm not going to apologise for destroying Livingston."

"You said you were sorry about my brother."

"That's different."

My jaw aches, my teeth gritted. "You can't have one without the other."

"Yes, I can. I'm sorry about… I'm sorry your… *I'm sorry I*

killed your brother. But not for Livingston."

She leaps to her feet.

And so we come to the end.

I roll backwards off the log in a hiss of sand. My finger tightens on the trigger of the Glock.

She'll be dead before she touches me.

17

Anita stares at me, frozen where she's jumped to her feet, her pulse fluttering in the hollow of her throat. I blink, expecting her to be diving at me with bared teeth and fisted hands. She watches me instead, not breathing. I sigh, and she flinches.

The gun slips back into my holster.

"Did you think I was going to attack you?" she says, a wobble in her voice.

I cock my head. "I never know with you."

Truth. She never reacts how I think she will. No gloating, no feminine wiles. She hasn't even tried that hard to escape.

Yet.

A burst of gunfire rattles in the distance.

"Get in the pod," I say.

She meekly climbs in without mouthing off but glowers when I scoop up the ropes.

How quickly she recovers to pout at me.

I smirk and bind her ankles and wrists. She wriggles against my grip but doesn't pull away.

"I don't like being tied up," she says.

"Yeah, who does?"

"Oh, some people do."

I snort.

A sex joke? Images flash in my head before I can stop them…

Crap. Must not think about sex. It's probably what she intended.

I slide away to hide my expression, gathering clothes and a soap capsule from the rucksack. "Stay in the pod with the door shut."

"Afraid I'll see you naked?"

God, that face. Insolent eyes, sulking mouth. The haughty tone makes me want to bite her.

Bite her? You mean strangle her, right?

Right.

Living in proximity to the Borderlanders has turned me into an animal.

"I don't care if you see me naked. It's the grabbing weapons and shooting me while I'm naked that I'm worried about." I force a grin, trying to ignore a pressure building in my gut.

Maybe all the bugs I've eaten are finally disagreeing with me.

The portal hisses shut. I pile my clean clothes on the beach, weapons and control pad balanced on top. A survey of the trees confirms we're alone. I glance at the pod. The door is shut, no face peeking through.

Why haven't I locked it? I'm testing her. To see if she'll try to escape. Or succumb to the temptation of seeing me naked.

No. The escape thing. Just the escape thing.

I shake my head and strip off. "Dylan, what the hell am I doing? My own prisoner isn't afraid of me. How can I—ah, *crap!*"

The icy water nips at my feet. Goosebumps race up my legs and tighten my shoulders. I wash quickly, dunking my head then sloshing back out. I dress in my navy combats—nicely repaired—and the green t-shirt Anita wore yesterday, washed and dried in the sun.

A hint of almond and something else. Cherry?

Why am I sniffing her t-shirt?

Jesus. No man's land has really scrambled my brain.

I crawl into the pod. Anita lies on her back, frowning at the ceiling. Green eyes flick to me and away, a faint pink tinging her high cheekbones.

"Are you blushing?"

She frowns harder at the ceiling. "No."

What was she doing, picturing me naked?

We eat dinner in stubborn silence. Fresh-caught rabbit, peas, fried chanterelles and cattail flower spikes, roasted and tasting like corn on the cob then a dessert of blackberries and coffee.

Better food than when I was in Livingston.

With little else to do, we resume our positions under the sleeping bag. Side to side, her tied up, a polite gap between us.

I can't go on like this. Dancing around the real issue. We aren't freaking camping out here for fun. She has to tell me. I have to know what Wick did to her. Whether I coax or shake it out of her, she has some talking to do.

"Blake?" Soft, tentative voice.

"What?"

"What did you do—before the rebellion?"

I turn my head. Serious eyes meet mine. This close, there's more detail. A darker green borders the iris, the jade flecked with gold and bronze.

Pretty.

How long have I been staring at her?

I clear my throat. "I was a fitness instructor."

She sniggers, amusement bringing out the gold. "Of course you were."

"What's that supposed to mean?"

Her chest hitches.

What is so damn funny?

"Clientele dominated by women?"

Well, yeah. I promised myself not to be sleazy and sleep with a client, otherwise my bed would never have been empty. Though most of them were married. It didn't stop them strutting around in their tight tops, bending over at the slightest opportunity, asking me to show them the best position to stretch in breathy voices, hoping I'd touch them. Their gaze never on my bloody face.

But faithless women turn me off.

There was one. Single. Gorgeous. Turquoise eyes and a compact little body. She quit my class and we spent a very enjoyable weekend at her place. God, her stamina…

Crap.

I cross my arms and bend my legs, lifting the sleeping bag off my hips. "I had male clients, too."

"Oh, I'm sure you did. And were most of them gay?"

"Gay? How the hell should I know?"

She wheezes and waves her bound hands. "Nothing. Forget I said it."

"And what were you? Movie star? Supermodel?"

She hiccups, scrubbing her face. "Recruitment consultant."

It doesn't match the picture in my head. The superior attitude, people scurrying to her beck and call, adoring men at her feet.

"What do you miss most from back then? You know, the normal stuff?"

What's with the questions—hoping we'll be friends and I'll decide not to kill her? Forcing me to see her as something other than the person who murdered my brother.

"What do I miss? Everything. Not being shot at. The ability to travel the world." I pause. "Ice cream."

"I miss movies. What?" she says to my snort. "You think that's worse than ice cream? 'Yippie-ki-yay, motherfucker.'"

I laugh, surprising myself. "Of course you quote that one. It may be ancient but there's swearing."

"It's not ancient. It's a classic."

"I thought the classics were all in black and white."

She rolls her eyes. "You might as well compare cave paintings to digital art."

"Oh, so you're a movie snob?"

"And what do you like? Gentle animation about fluffy bunnies and unicorns?"

"Something a bit more modern. Computer graphics. Super-heroes."

"You're entitled to your opinion. Wrong, but you're entitled to it."

"Woman, you are something else."

She grins and an ache flares in my chest. I stare at the ceiling.

"It's hard, isn't it?" she says. "Remembering what life was like before, when we could actually be happy. When we weren't alone, surviving one day to the next."

"I wasn't alone," I whisper.

She meets my gaze, and flinches.

That's right, baby. I wasn't alone until you came along and stomped over everything.

I turn my back and pretend to sleep.

18

A warm weight curls against me. Hands push at my chest. My arm tightens across slim shoulders.

What is Anita trying to do—hug me or get the weapons?

Well, she touched me first.

I slide my hand down her back and cup her arse. Her weight jerks away. I open my eyes.

She bites her lip, her gaze darting to the side. "Would you believe I was trying to reach the weapons and fell?"

"On top of me?"

"Fine. How about you cuddle me in your sleep?"

"Seems unlikely."

She thrusts her bound hands under my nose. "Untie me. I need some air."

I wrap my fingers around her wrists. She tugs against my hold. I sit up and her slender hands brush my chest. Her eyes widen; her breathing quickens. She pulls harder and excitement curls in my stomach.

"I thought you wanted me to untie you," I say.

"So hurry up and do it."

I like this panic. The desperation of cornered prey, aware of how easily I could pin her to the ground and have her squirming under—

106

Nope.

The rope flops to the floor, the skin of her wrists reddened but not broken. I hook my arm in her bent calves and yank to straighten her legs. She yelps, slapping her palm on the floor instead of toppling into the covers. I shift towards her feet.

"I can untie my ankles, thank you," she sniffs.

"Why are you so twitchy?"

"I'm not twitchy."

"Whatever you say."

She scowls and picks at the knot. Her frown deepens, colour flaring in her cheeks.

"Would you like some assistance?" I say in my blandest voice.

"*Please*," she growls.

Such a sore loser.

I reach for the rope binding her ankles, and freeze. Her feet are bare, delicate, with a graceful arch. And pitted, thickened skin where her toenails should be.

Wick ripped them out. All of them.

My throat closes. A shaking finger strokes Anita's nailbeds.

The area is rough but hardening, the nails growing back.

I touch each toe.

I lost a nail once while training for a marathon. The raw bed was excruciating, socks and shoes an impossibility.

One nail that had fallen off, not been yanked out by pliers.

Anita curls her toes. "Stop that."

Commanding words, breathy voice.

I unwrap the rope from her ankles. She scrambles for the portal as if frantic to get away from me.

"Anita. You might want to wait until I unlock it."

Her shoulders hunch.

Is she trembling?

I click the button on the control pad. "You are free to go."

"Neither of us is free," she snarls and bolts outside.

Her fading footsteps crunch into the forest.

Part of me hopes she'll keep walking. The other part wants to chase after her and make her talk. Or take her in my arms and—

Nope. You're not supposed to be attracted to her, you moron.

Dylan would be ashamed. I scoff at the disloyalty of others but here I am having cosy chats with his killer, teasing her, letting her live.

Feeling sorry for her.

In my defence, she's the first person I've gotten close to in two months who doesn't want to eat me.

Loneliness does crazy things.

I climb out of the pod and sit on the log facing the trees. Anita returns after ten minutes and holds her hand out, two eggs balanced on her palm.

"Brought breakfast."

She's calmer, no flush, the wild light gone from her eyes. She fries the eggs with mushrooms and slivers of potato. After washing the dishes, she settles in the sand and peeks at me.

"What?"

She clears her throat. "When you, ah, jumped me... I was going somewhere."

"So?"

"So... I was travelling to the coast. To Eyemouth—to find a boat—to escape the country and... I think you should come with me."

"Woman, what the hell are you talking about?"

"The rest of the world might be okay. Someone's out there at least. If we leave Scotland, we could be free. Have a real life again."

My hand fists in the sand, my heart thumping.

Does that mean my mum is alive? Could I see her again?

Sure, and tell her I've broken my promise and Dylan is dead and Anita killed him. Oh, and I wanted to hurt her but now I think I like her. Can't see my mum having a problem there.

"How do you know that?" I say.

"A doctor—my friend—in Fellhill. She heard a broadcast on a radio. Okay, it was two years ago, but it's got to be better than this."

Anita is only thinking of herself. If we escape and the world is civilised, shooting her will be frowned upon. She'll ditch me at the first opportunity. Or she's lying about all of it.

"We're not going anywhere until I've decided what I'm doing with you," I say.

"What you're doing with me? Are you fucking serious? We could be free of this shit!"

"You! *You* could be free! I can't be free because of what you did!"

She bares her teeth and her eyes flash. "Then judge my worthiness on the damn road, oh mighty lord justice. Just hurry the hell up. And quit acting like you've never killed anyone. You may not have killed my sister but you'll have killed someone's family."

"Keep talking," I growl, my hand tightening on the Glock at my waist. "Maybe I'll choose the option that'll shut you up quicker."

Her hands ball into fists. She rises slowly to her feet despite her obvious fury—learns fast this one—and stalks to the edge of the pool to glower over the water, her back to me.

It'd be so easy to raise my gun, aim at her head and squeeze the trigger. She'd flop face down in the shallows and that would be that.

Cowardly, though. If I decide to execute her, I want to see her eyes. Watch the understanding dawn. The denial, the anger, the fear. Acceptance.

I guess I am a bit psychotic after all.

"Are there fish in here?" The words are clipped, her spine stiff.

"Yes."

"Can we catch some?"

Why not? It would be cathartic to do something productive instead of slaughtering her.

"You go in the water. I'll gut."

She is not getting anywhere near a knife.

She changes into a pair of shorts, her legs long and toned, not that I notice. She crafts a hook and line from a shoelace and a hawthorn branch, baiting it with worms and wading into the pool close to the water lilies.

She's still wearing my navy t-shirt, probably too stubborn to take it off since I mentioned it.

I drag a flat stone closer to the water's edge and sit next to it, my knife ready. The sun bakes the top of my head, a light breeze rippling my clothes. Anita tenses, easing her fingers into the pool, her other hand tugging on the line. She scoops up a grayling but it thrashes in her hands, splattering her. She turns to me and I smirk at the water sparkling in her hair and running down her face.

Not such a fun idea now, is it?

I react too slowly to the glint in her eyes.

She lobs the fish. It slaps my chest and flops to the sand. I gape at her and she laughs.

"Goddammit, woman." I peel the cold wetness of my t-shirt off my skin and lift the grayling, bashing its head with the handle of my knife.

Anita recasts, chuckling to herself. I gut the fish, pretending it's her. She catches another and I brace but the woman can throw. It hits my shoulder, splashing water on my face. Frustration builds as each slippery body slithers past my grip and soaks me. Anita shakes with laughter and staggers out of the pool, resting her hands on her knees and gasping for breath.

Okay, so I hoped the fishing would be a release for me, not her.

"You look damp," she says between giggles.

Delight changes her from beautiful to stunning.

I cock an eyebrow. "You seem to be enjoying yourself."

"Somehow, I am."

God, I suck at terrorising women. You'd think I would've learned something from Wick.

Anita straightens and scrubs her face, smearing grayling goop on her cheek. My turn to laugh. I pull my t-shirt off, the material wet and distinctly fishy. Anita's gaze shifts downward. The heat of it tightens my gut, a spear of arousal hardening my body.

What a twisted pair we are.

"You're blushing."

"It's a hot day," she says, her voice doing that wobbling thing.

I smirk. Her eyes narrow. She raises her chin and stalks around me.

Oh, she does not like being attracted to me, either. Excellent.

I gather the fillets from the rock and follow her but she's stopped, staring at me with a horrified expression.

She must have seen the scars on my back.

"What?" I say harshly. "You think Wick reserved torture for his prisoners? He was just as happy abusing his own people."

She seems unaware of her fingertips rubbing over her heart, her eyes all for me. Dazed and dark and… Sad?

"You, too?" she says. "You've been in there?"

"Twice. The whipping was for punching one of Wick's guards. He bragged about raping a prisoner and cutting her open. I don't even remember hitting him."

Why am I telling her this? She never tells me a bloody thing.

"I'm sorry," she whispers and her breath hitches.

Great. She pities me.

I shake my head and walk to the smoker I built in the trees, cramming pieces of cut wood into the space. She trails after me.

"If Wick was cruel to you guys, why did nobody stop him?"

Sure. Like it was easy.

I flick my lighter and flames lick the branches, tension singing in my shoulders.

"We were terrified of him; we'd do anything to stay on his good side." My thoughts flash back to that one day. "Almost anything. Funny how much you tolerate if you think you're going to win. It made everything else bearable."

She shivers and hugs herself.

Good. She's finally getting it.

I seal the smoker with rocks. "Wick had enough followers to protect him. No guarantee once he was removed someone worse wouldn't take his place. And what would that make me? A leader-assassinating traitor. This war had enough of those at the start."

But I wanted to kill him. Every time he paraded a new victim through his torture chamber. I was paralysed by the fear of what would happen if I were caught. So I watched and ignored and tried to forget like everybody else.

I face Anita and she scrubs her cheeks.

Crying? Nah, surely not.

"I killed my leader," she says.

My eyes widen.

Is that why she's out here? Was it—who's the leader of Soldiers of the Lost?—Simmons?

"Which one?" I say.

"Marshall."

The ground shifts under my feet.

Wrong again. She can't have been one of his whores. He pampered them and didn't force them to fight.

"Why?" I say.

She drops her gaze to her nail-less toes, half-hidden in the sandy soil. No stubborn pout this time.

"Why?" I say, softer, a weird tightness in my chest.

"He sent me to Fellhill to die."

Why would he do that? Wasn't he her brother-in-law?

She sighs. "Marshall demanded I sleep with him but I refused."

We walk back to the pod, the heat of the sun blazing after the shade of the trees. I struggle not to stumble into her, my mind whirling and messing with my coordination.

"Wasn't he family?"

"He was *not* fucking family," she says. "Look, my point is—coming from someone who's been called a traitor more than once—assassinating your leader doesn't make you one. Some people deserve to die."

I can't help a smile. "So you decide who's worthy enough to

live?"

She walked right into that one.

"When they're trying to kill me or demanding something that isn't theirs, I guess I do."

So why hasn't she tried to kill me?

She flops in the sand and leans against a log. I sit opposite her, stretching my legs and wriggling to get comfortable.

"Who called you a traitor? Soldiers of the Lost when they thought you destroyed the dragon?"

She jumps. "I don't want to talk about it."

Goddammit. I'm finally learning something. Okay, I'll try gentle, coaxing. See where it gets me.

I let sand trickle from my palm. "You can't blame me for being interested. Wick was a sadist but he left us alone for the most part, as long as he had prisoners to keep him entertained. Sounds like your time has been pretty awful."

"Recently, it has."

"Oh, come on. You can't say that and give me nothing."

"Sure I can."

That mouth. *Infuriating.*

She clears her throat. "I tell you everything now, you'll get bored and decide to shoot me. Think I'll keep my secrets."

She *is* afraid. Not afraid I'll hurt her but something else.

And why does that send arousal tingling to the tip of my cock?

I tried not to become one of Wick's delinquents but it seems I've been tainted anyway.

Anita mumbles something about heat stroke and scuttles to the pod.

19

What do I really know about this woman? She was Revolutionary Front's prisoner when we captured her. Wick sent four men to find her, two came back. Wick tortured her for five days, including ripping out her toenails and trying, but failing, to rape her. In the two weeks before Calders was destroyed, she was sent to die in Fellhill. Soldiers of the Lost took her prisoner and made her steal the dragon. A woman tried to frame her for destroying it. Was that why she left Fellhill? Did no man's land seem safer?

Called a traitor more than once.

It must have been Soldiers of the Lost. And Marshall? He wouldn't have liked her refusal. Why didn't she sleep with him for an easier, if somewhat incestuous, life? Most women would have.

I guess she isn't like most women.

She's a fighter. A bloody good one. Why hasn't she fought me? She could've grabbed a rock during her huff in the trees and brained me with it. She didn't have to get close. She can throw. Instead, she lets me berate her, tie her up.

Lets me? snarls my ego. *I have the strength to handle one woman, thank you very much.*

Yeah, one who isn't trying to escape. Or hurt me. And why

is that?

Maybe she does feel bad.

A soft whimper comes from the pod. I sit up.

"No, *please*." Anita's voice, so broken and lost.

I reach the portal in two strides. She lies on top of the covers, her eyes closed, hands held as if warding something off. Sweat glistens on her upper lip and pools in the hollow of her throat.

I crawl in beside her and grip her shoulders. "Anita, wake up."

She slaps at my arms, digging her heels into the floor and arching her back. I push down and she bucks underneath me, a whine trapped in her throat.

She's going to hurt herself.

I stretch over her, trying to keep her still. "Ssh, Anita. It's okay. You're safe."

Safe? Really?

Shut up.

She thrashes, such strength in her lithe body. Her fist catches me in the corner of the mouth. I pin her arms.

"Dammit, Anita, *wake up!* You're having a nightmare."

She gasps awake. Wide eyes filled with fear and shame snap to mine. Welling tears magnify the green and gold and bronze.

"Oh god, are you real?" she says.

I'm close enough to feel her breath and drown in the feverish heat of her skin. I relax my grip, pushing my weight off her.

Her distress does funny things to my stomach.

"I'm real. It was a nightmare."

Her face pales. "Going to be sick."

She scrambles out of the pod, sand hissing as she stumbles away. My gut clenches in sympathy at the noise of her throwing up. I touch my swollen lip and a tiny bead of blood trembles on my finger.

That was one hell of a nightmare. It doesn't take a genius to figure out who'd have the starring role. I suffer them, too— black eyes and sharp, blood-encrusted fingernails grabbing me from the dark.

I force myself outside despite being the last person Anita will want to see. She shivers in the sand beside the logs, her knees hugged to her chest.

Vulnerable.

"Are you okay?" I perch on the opposite log instead of scooping her into my arms.

Christ, a female in trouble and I get all sentimental.

"It was Wick." Her breath shudders at the name. "In my nightmare. Haven't had one in a while."

"I'm not helping, am I?"

"Not so much."

I lick the blood from the corner of my mouth in a burst of copper. She heaves herself upright, leaning back against the log.

No cowering for this one.

"Sorry I hit you."

She's apologising to me?

"Surprised you haven't done it before."

Her tentative laugh makes the strange protectiveness worse. She stares at her lap, massaging her injured arm and stretching her fingers.

"I'm sorry. For everything." Her eyes flick to me and dart away. "I'm sorry for your brother, for Livingston. I was hurt. *Furious.* You broke me. I thought you deserved it. Fooled myself you were all like him. I wanted to hurt you, as I'd been hurt. But I regretted it later."

I wanted the same after Dylan. Her to hurt, as I'd been hurt.

My chest fills with sorrow, tightening my throat and prickling my eyes.

Thankfully, Anita isn't looking at me since I'm too upset to hide it.

Missing my brother too damn much.

"Will you tell me what Wick did?" I choke out.

Her head snaps up, a snarl on her lips.

Lashing out to protect herself.

"*Please.* I have to know my brother's death wasn't for nothing. That you were driven to it. Please."

Her expression crumples. "I've never told anyone."

"I know what that's like."

"Your second time in the torture chamber?"

"First, actually. The whipping was the second time." My hand bats at the air. "That's a horror story for another day. Tell me yours first."

She bows her head and swallows hard. "What was your brother's name?"

Deflecting or gathering courage? Understandable. I haven't told anyone about my Wick experiences, either. Not in full.

Too humiliating.

"Dylan." God, his name hurts. "Dylan O'Riley."

She meets my eyes without flinching. "How was he in Livingston? Did he join Nationless because you were family?"

"He was visiting. Came to convince me to return to Ireland, where our mother lived. He was stranded by the bombs." I should have made him go home. It was my fault he came. My fault he stayed. My fault he died. "The last thing I said to my mother before we were cut off was a promise to keep him safe. But maybe she's dead, too. Maybe I'll never have to tell her I failed. I don't know which would be worse."

My hands cover my face and muffle my voice.

I can't look at her. I've shown her too much already.

What a pussy.

"The worst part about the torture was Wick didn't want anything. No information, no secrets. Nothing but me begging for my life. And I don't beg. Not for anyone." Anita's voice hardens.

I raise my head but she doesn't meet my gaze.

"He recognised me. He changed. He was Daniel, the party leader, not Wick, the monster. I thought... I thought he wouldn't hurt me."

"We had no Daniel, only Wick," I say. "In the beginning, we thought it was the head injury. Of course he'd want vengeance. But then we realised he was a different person. Darker. And he enjoyed the torture too much to stop."

"Oh, I know how much he enjoyed it. He beat me with a rubber truncheon and he *whistled*." Tears glisten in her eyes. "I still hear the noise it made. Sounded the same as the metal bat I used to pulverise his face. But there's literally a lot of shit to get through before that part." Her attempt at a laugh cracks. "The next day, I was hauled from my cell by some muscle-bound goliath—"

"Doolly," I growl, my hands fisted.

The monstrous bastard. Smug in his position as torture guard. Loving his power over the defenceless. Joining in to rape and torture the pretty ones. He must've been thrilled when he saw Anita. I never regretted punching him despite the whipping it earned me. I only wished he were alive in the aftermath of Anita's departure so I could've murdered him.

I shake myself and gesture for her to continue.

It's not the time to be distracted by Doolly the steroid monster.

"He strapped me to a chair and Wick electrocuted me. Fainted the first time. Felt everything the second."

She tells me everything. How the electric shocks made her soil herself. How Wick pulled out her toenails and some of her teeth. Punished her with more of the rubber truncheon and electric belt. Drowned her, beat her. Whipped her.

Just like me.

He'd wrapped his long fingers around her throat and squeezed. And he tried to rape her. Brutalised, debased, humiliated, she surrendered. Tired of fighting. Wanting to die.

She doesn't seem to notice the tears sliding down her cheeks. I find myself on my feet and moving towards her but stop, frowning at the electrigun strapped to my arm, the Glock on my hip.

It's an Oscar-worthy performance if it's a lie. I don't think it is—who can fake that kind of despair?—but…

I place the weapons on the log out of reach and sit beside her. She curls against me, her warm breath tickling my neck. Her hand slides across my chest, her fingers gripping my ribs and pulling me closer.

I really should have put on a t-shirt. The soft tears dripping on my collarbone are unbearably distracting. Each one resonates in my gut.

I wrap my arms around her hitching shoulders.

No wonder she was furious. Wick broke her and she could never forgive herself. Or the faction that allowed it to happen.

Her lips move against my neck and jolt my pulse.

"Afterwards, I flew back to Calders and spent a week in the

medical centre. Seizures, cardiac arrhythmias, malnutrition, nightmares. Not to mention my wobbly mental state and the fact most people came to believe I was a traitor, thanks to Marshall, which probably wasn't helped by me shooting my sister's best friend as soon as I stepped out the dragon."

So not tucked up in bed, pampered and comforted, but hurt and alone.

"He gave me an ultimatum—sleep with him or die a traitor. If I'd known Soldiers of the Lost were to be his method of execution, maybe I would've slept with him. But probably not. That sex-obsessed bastard didn't deserve to touch me."

I stroke her hair and her shudders ease under my hands.

"So he threw me to the wolves in Fellhill."

Jesus. How did she not go insane?

An awful tension leaches from my body, draining months of frustration and anger.

It's enough. For now, it's enough.

Dylan would've understood.

"Thank you," I whisper into Anita's hair.

"Oh, my pleasure," she huffs. "When you want a horror story, just ask. I have plenty."

I bite my lip, her breath scalding my chest and caressing my stomach.

"Always with the sass."

"Stops me from falling apart. Most of the time."

Tears sparkle in her lashes and wet her reddened cheeks. She scrubs her face, sliding out of my arms. I stop myself from hugging her tighter. She cocks an eyebrow towards the weapons on the log.

I shrug. "I can never tell how you'll react."

"I don't think I'm ruthless enough to grab a gun when you're being consolatory."

"So I should go back to being an arsehole?"

"Soon. Just give me another minute."

I chuckle and she rewards me with a smirk, her shields slipping into place. The wicked glint returns to her eyes and distracts me.

It's my only defence for being caught off-guard.

Sand slithers and Anita's face freezes.

"You picked the wrong day to go camping, you faction-loving bastards," a man says.

20

Shit-fuck-balls.

Did I say that out loud?

Two men, stained clothes, questionable hygiene—Borderlanders. The stockier man swipes the electrigun and Glock off the log, tossing them behind him. A creepy smile twists his mouth, his eyes unfocused, drifting over our camp but not alighting on anything for more than a second.

"Move over there," the taller man barks at me, gesturing with a scuffed Browning. "Keep your hands where I can see 'em."

I really wish I'd put on a t-shirt.

I stand slowly, Anita mirroring me, and move closer to the squat man. His pale eyes assesses my approach before his gaze floats over the pool.

"I see why you wanted some privacy." The tall man sneers. "Does she fuck as good as she looks? Bet she does."

Like I'd know. I'm not a savage who shags everything with a pulse.

The stocky man kicks the back of my leg. "On your knees, pretty-boy. Hands on your head."

I drop to the sand. The tall man presses his gun to Anita's temple, fisting his hand in her hair and yanking, stretching her throat, her pulse trapped and fluttering beneath the pale skin.

"Bet you have to chase the men from this 'un."

The man slides the barrel down her cheek and neck then pushes it into the side of her breast. She bares her teeth and the man laughs.

"Bend over and spread your legs."

"Fuck you."

"Oh, honey, you're about to."

He shoves the gun to her head, forcing her lower and kicking her ankle to widen her legs. He uses her hair as a leash and steps behind her.

"Hold your arms out."

He folds his tall body over her back, his filthy hands slithering along her outstretched arms to grope her breasts. I twitch with the need to throw myself at him and break his fingers. He grips her hips, thrusting against her arse. She braces a hand on the ground.

"You should see her," the man beside me says, his mouth split in a grin. "Angel-face is pissed."

She's not pissed. How many men have tried to rape her? Marshall, Wick. Others?

The war is no medium for restraint.

I'll kill the bastard for touching her.

The hips thrust again. "Good. I like the ones that fight."

So did Wick. Breaking them was so much more satisfying.

Anita's eyes meet mine, and my heart thuds painfully. She drops her gaze, her cheeks flushed.

"Let's unwrap you and see what delights we have in store." The tall man tugs her upright. "Take the top off."

She glances at me.

I have to do something. I can't kneel here and watch her be raped. The man beside me is unarmed.

"Your little boyfriend can't help you," the tall man says. "Do what I tell you or Gavin will cut 'im."

A knife as long as my forearm appears in Gavin's hand.

Well, crap.

"And I'll shoot you in the leg and fuck you anyway." The barrel aims at her kneecap. "Top. *Off*."

Her eyes spark but she jerks her t-shirt off and flings it on the sand. I should show solidarity by not looking but I can't seem to help it.

I barely hear the man say, "Oh, what a pity. Just as well you have great tits. I'm a tits and ass man."

It's not the black bra that grips my attention, as intriguing as the contents may be. It's the scars. An old bullet wound on her left shoulder, roughly circular. A long, pink line down her belly. Neat, surgical. I can't see her back but it'll be similar to mine, with raised ridges of tissue where the whip bit her skin.

How many people have hurt this woman? How many arseholes have laid hands on her, abused her, forced her to do what they wanted?

I'm no different. Condemning her reaction to her torture. Labelling her a murderer.

Dylan was collateral damage. She didn't target him. She had no idea he was even there. Blasting an attacking jet out of her path probably threw it into the house.

And how many loved ones have I killed? I destroyed a chunk of Lowkirk during the assault where we captured Anita. Mowed down fleeing soldiers from the comparative safety of my aircraft.

It's a war. People die.

I focus on Anita's face, trying to show how damn sorry I am for dragging her into this. Her lovely eyes lock on mine.

"Shorts next, beautiful."

She jumps, her attention returning to the dead-man-walking beside her. Her hand falls to her waistband. Muddy brown eyes track the movement, a tongue flicking over scabbed lips. My fingers dig into the top of my head and rage boils in my stomach.

"You're going to regret this," Anita says in her haughty voice.

It soothes the ache in my chest.

Yes. Fight him. Torment him with that stubborn mouth. When he's suitably distracted, I'll ram his rotten teeth down his throat.

The man grins. "I doubt it."

She kicks the shorts off to reveal matching black underwear. Instead of hunching and covering herself, she raises her chin and scowls at the man.

God, she is glorious. Strong, confident. A warrior.

Why am I only realising this now?

Too obsessed by my own pain to notice hers. Self-righteous dick.

So I lost someone? Find me someone who hasn't.

Wick's brutality killed Dylan and ruined Nationless. Our punishment for doing nothing while he tortured hundreds. Anita reacted as anyone would have. As I would have. If she left us whole, we would've attacked Calders to reclaim the dragon. She was protecting herself.

Because no one else would.

I shut my eyes, disgusted at myself. Fingers weave into my hair and tug hard.

"Open your eyes, lover-boy, you get to watch," a voice giggles in my ear. "Or I cut off your eyelids and force you. You choose."

Gavin waves the knife under my nose in a waft of cheesy,

unwashed skin.

I'll rip him apart. Stomp on his creepy, smiley face.

The blast of a gunshot punches into my chest.

Anita!

21

The grip disappears from my hair and the knife droops away from my face. Anita punches the tall man, his nose bursting in a bloody spray.

Unwounded. Fighting.

Help her, you jackass.

The tall man stumbles over the log and sits hard on his arse. Gavin steps towards them. I grab his wrist and pull myself to my feet.

His skin is sticky.

I keep one hand wrapped around his wrist and chop my fingers into the crook of his elbow to bend his arm.

His pale eyes widen, his mouth no longer smiling.

I ram the knife into the side of his neck and the blade scrapes bone, his fingers still clutching the handle.

Another gunshot.

I jerk the knife free, ripping out the front of Gavin's throat in a gout of red. He flops to the ground. The tall man is sprawled on his back, his feet propped on the log he tripped over, a wound seeping in his forehead. Anita stands, the Browning raised and pointed at me in a two-handed, straight-armed grip. Relief weakens my knees. Her eyes blaze.

She doesn't lower the gun.

The knife slips from my fingers and thuds into the sand.

I am a stupid, soft-hearted idiot. How can I expect her forgiveness when I haven't given her mine? Of course she seizes the first opportunity to rid herself of me. I'm like everyone else—judgemental, prejudiced, self-obsessed.

Abusive.

"Do it," I say. "I deserve it."

I watch my death on her face, in the tension in her muscles, her knuckles white around the gun.

There'll be no more worrying about getting eaten by an abomination or Borderlanders. No more grief. I kept my promise to Stig and tried to live but I lost myself in no man's land.

At least this way, Anita and I both get some peace.

She sucks in a breath. I shut my eyes and hope it won't hurt.

"Blake?" Warm fingers curl on my bare shoulder.

I flinch and my eyes snap open.

Maybe she wants a closer shot. To jam the barrel in my neck and pull the trigger.

The Browning hangs at her side, pressed to her thigh. A lock of hair drifts across her cheek, teased by the wind and golden in the sunlight.

Of course she does the opposite of what I say. I should have told her *not* to kill me.

She opens her mouth but I can't take another apology. I may yell at her to show how much of a tough man I am.

Though crying seems an embarrassing possibility.

"I'm"—I clear my throat—"I miss him."

Whoops. I meant to tell her I'm fine. Call her woman since it annoys her.

She swallows. "I know. I'm sorry."

Dammit.

I frown at her chest, desperately trying for anger instead of some girly crap.

Why can't she be a screeching, malicious bitch?

It'd be easier to hate her.

Her dog-tags swing below her breasts, the beaded chains framed by black material and porcelain skin. I jerk my eyes upwards. A small line bisects the scar on her shoulder. I fist my hand to avoid stroking it.

The last thing she'll want is for me to touch her.

She steps into me, and I stiffen. Her arms circle my shoulders, her cheek pressed to mine. Exactly my height.

Crap. I'm a sucker for a hug.

My hands slide around her waist, preoccupied by the edge of her underwear beneath my fingertips. I follow it to the small of her back and find the roughness of scars.

More extensive than mine.

Wick didn't whip me for long. Only enough to teach me a lesson and get himself excited.

But he was brutal with Anita.

My back burns in sympathy, remembering the terrible pain despite the passing years.

Gentle pressure pulls her closer.

I swear I only mean for it to be comforting but her breath catches in her throat. I bury my nose in her hair, the scent of her drowning the sensible part of my brain screaming *what the hell are you doing!?*

She wants me. Reacts to my touch. Her stunned face when I took my t-shirt off. Blushes if I look at her.

She trembles in my arms and her skin scorches me. My hand traces the scars on her back, caressing from shoulder to hip beneath the silken weight of her hair. Her shivers tingle through me and curl in my stomach.

"Blake, wait…" That haughty voice, breathy and strangled. "Blake, we have to go. Might be others."

She wriggles and eases out of my arms. I grip her waist, not wanting the hug to end—the closeness—but her scars distract me. My finger traces them.

"Wick didn't do these," I manage to say, my voice little more than a growl.

She shakes her head, her hair tumbling over her shoulders. "No. Not Wick."

She stares at me, her eyes wide, lips parted. The copperiness of blood finally penetrates.

What the fuck am I doing?

I release her so fast, she stumbles. Nausea roils in my gut. I gather the weapons out of habit and pack up camp, avoiding her gaze.

I don't need to see the disgust.

Just another man wanting to screw her.

I forge a path into the trees, leaving her the rucksack.

I deserve it if she runs. But I have the weapons. I should give her a gun, set her free.

I've done enough damage.

What the hell was I thinking? She was almost *raped* for Christ's sake. I have no business touching her, whether she hugged me first or not. I should be protecting her, not pawing at her in her underwear. Do I have no self-control?

Two months without sex and I turn into a pervert. Wick would be proud.

Fists bunched, I increase my pace to outrun the shame. The landscape passes in a blur of green and brown, no destination in mind. Anita's footsteps quicken. I hunch, expecting a blow.

I won't defend myself. The pain can't be worse than how I already feel.

No punch connects.

Why isn't she cursing at me? Maybe I get one pass for despicable behaviour. Dead brother and all.

A valley. A river. I climb to a plateau of ancient trees, each breath tearing my lungs.

I'm running out of names to call myself. Slut, delinquent, sav—

Crack.

I turn too slowly.

22

A weight slams into me and knocks me to the grass. The thud seems too loud, hissing through the vegetation.

Is Anita okay?

I roll, struggling beneath the heavy body sprawled across me. Only when I'm sitting in her lap, the rucksack propping her up, my hands gripping her arms, do I realise it's Anita.

Pale face, no resistance.

A muffled whack draws my gaze over my shoulder. A huge log, draped in ivy and bound by rope to the canopy, swings into the trunk of a tree. Maroon stains the rough bark in rivulets.

"Saved your life," Anita croaks.

Why didn't she let the trap crush me?

Blake pancake. Easy way out.

Her eyes glisten. A fine tremble transfers between us.

I'm pretty sure it isn't me.

Pretty sure.

"Are you crying?" I say.

She sniffs and ducks her head. "No. That would be ridiculous."

I brush my fingers across her cheek and capture a single, sparkling tear. The weird pressure returns to my gut.

She saved my life. After everything I've done.

I swallow. "Something in your eye?"

"Right. Makes more sense."

"And while you had this thing in your eye, you saved my life?"

"I don't want you to die."

"Why not?"

"What do you mean 'why not'?"

I shrug but don't pull off the nonchalance. "I'm keeping you prisoner. Making you relive difficult parts of your life. Touching you when I said I wouldn't."

She licks her lips, a flush tinting her cheekbones and highlighting the beauty of her face.

"My fault. Forgot I was in my underwear."

"You forgot?"

"You were hurting."

"So you were more concerned with hugging me than putting your clothes on? Despite what might have happened?"

"Yes. Wait—no." She sighs. "I don't know. You confuse me."

The pressure expands into my chest and does crazy things to my heartbeat.

"You're confused? You make it very hard not to touch you."

"You *want* to touch me?"

I smirk. "Woman, have you not been paying attention?"

"But, what about—"

I press my fingers to her lips. So soft, so warm. Too easy to get distracted.

"I forgive you."

How could I not? She's been abused by the people closest to her. Tortured to breaking point. And the scars. Who else has hurt her? What's a little grief compared to the crap she's suffered?

She knows exactly what losing a sibling is like.

"No you don't," she says. "You can't. You're lonely. Confused."

"You're the one crying because I almost died."

She scowls and jerks her face away from my hand, my fingers stroking her bottom lip without any urging from my brain. The haughtiness returns, stubbornness pouting her mouth.

Infuriatingly sexy.

"Maybe you've convinced yourself you want me. You'll feel guilty after. Angry at me. I'll be the one who gets hurt. Because I killed your brother and you can't possibly forgive me for that."

I can't keep from flinching but she's wrong about the other stuff.

"And if I still say I have?"

"Men will say, and do, anything to get what they want. I won't be manipulated this time. I'm not a goddamn conquest."

Another one. A bastard who got close to her. Held her, touched her.

"Someone hurt you before," I say softly. "Someone you trusted."

"None of your business. Get off me."

I force myself to lean back, put a little distance between us, instead of curling myself around her with a protective growl.

"Not until you tell me about it."

"I can make you move."

"You can try."

She twitches and I tense. She still catches me by surprise even though I know it's coming.

The woman has skills.

Her foot traps my leg. At the same time, she tilts her hips and grabs my arms. I topple sideways but use the extra weight of the rucksack to continue the roll, shoving her onto her chest. I press my body to the rucksack and pin her uninjured arm to the ground.

"Goddammit, Blake," she says.

I laugh at her indignation, a green eye glaring at me from the spill of her hair. I kneel between her thrashing legs and force them wider.

"If it makes you feel any better, you'd kick my arse if your arm were healed. And you didn't have the rucksack on."

She shakes the hair from her face, panting and dishevelled and unbearably cute. "I saved your life, quit being a dick."

"Tell me about the person who hurt you."

"Why?"

I have to know. Desperately. Immediately. Hearing about the people who've abused her makes it impossible for me to hurt her, too.

"Perhaps I want to know what's turned you into the fascinating woman you are today."

She bucks, somehow lifting herself a few inches.

Of course she won't surrender without a fight.

I jerk her arm and she thuds down with a wheeze.

"You're going to exhaust yourself," I say.

"Fuck you."

Ah, that mouth.

"Feeling better, are we?"

"The person who set the trap could come by at any moment. We don't have time for this."

I scan the forest but nothing moves between the trunks. The booby trap lies still against the tree.

"The quicker you tell me, the quicker we can leave."

"And then what?"

"Then you get to walk in front until you've calmed down and promise not to beat me up."

"That is a promise you will not be getting."

I laugh and lean my full weight on her, bringing my lips close to her ear. "I like fighting with you."

"His name was Gizzy," she blurts.

I instantly hate the guy. Who the hell calls themselves Gizzy?

A complete twat, that's who.

I lift myself clear of Anita and back up to lean on a tree, checking for other traps. She scrambles to her feet and shrugs off the rucksack. Her long legs carry her in a circle, her gaze fixed on the grass whispering against her boots.

She's still wearing my t-shirt.

"He captured me in Fellhill, treated me like a person instead of an enemy. Seemed kind, compassionate. Held me while I cried. Sound familiar?" She glares and stops mid-pivot. "Can I get a gun?"

I raise my eyebrows.

She huffs. "I think it's obvious I'm not going to kill you. I need one. I hate being unarmed and…"

"Vulnerable."

"Yes, fine—vulnerable."

Does being aroused by her vulnerability make me a sicko? Probably. I can't help it. She won't let many people see it. Hiding must be exhausting. I want her to know she doesn't have to be strong all the time. She can be herself.

I want her to trust me.

Christ, why don't I just marry her already?

I unbuckle the holster from my waist and hold out her Glock. Her eyes flick between it and me, her steps slow and precise.

"You think I'm going to attack you?"

She swipes the holster and retreats, her chin raised. "I never know with you."

I smirk. My words tossed back at me in her snooty voice.

She fastens the holster around her hips without any adjustment.

Dylan would piss himself at that.

His name causes a familiar ache in my stomach but it's not as raw. More like an ulcer than a blade to the gut.

The healing power of forgiveness. Who knew?

Anita removes the Glock from its holster and squeezes it in her hand, her knuckles bunching around it.

"You were saying?" I say before she starts hugging it.

She sighs and resumes her circuit. "Gizzy promised he wouldn't hurt me, said I could tell him about my torture when I was ready. I believed him. He was the first person I let myself get close to since this whole mess started."

I jerk forward. "Are you saying he was the only person you've had sex with this entire time, and recently?"

No intimacy in ten years? Impossible.

"What? Yes, he was the only one. Were you humping like rabbits in Livingston?"

"No, not like rabbits, no. Normal human beings."

She blushes and I grin at her discomfort.

How can a seasoned warrior have this innocence inside of her? Flustered and embarrassed about sex but more than capable of killing me.

A bewitching combination.

Yup, I'm a sicko.

"No wonder you believed everything he said." Laughter bubbles in my chest, a welcome release that makes my head light.

I've missed teasing someone.

"Fine, so I fucked him and lost all my senses. Happy?"

She's cute when she's mad.

"I'm sure that's not true. I can't imagine you ever let your guard down completely. Not even during an orgasm."

She hugs herself and frowns at her boots. "The woman who torched the dragon, he dumped her for me. Pretty much immediately, even when I was an enemy. That's why she framed me for it. Almost worked, too."

My amusement dies.

The guy hurt her. Tricked her. It isn't funny.

"Gizzy followed his leader in believing I'd done it. Destroyed the only thing I loved in the whole damn war. When I was sentenced to death, he was ordered to join the firing squad—"

"He wouldn't."

"—and would've blasted me to pieces if the stupid bitch hadn't stashed the petrol cans in her house. I was released. She was executed. Gizzy stayed in the line. I think he was the one who shot off half her face."

Her hand fists around the Glock, her knuckles blazing white. The rasp of her breath draws me closer.

How blind was the twat-nozzle? The way she speaks about the dragon shows how much she loved her. The softness of her face, the quiet awe. She never would've destroyed the machine.

"That's why I left Soldiers of the Lost. Couldn't live in Fellhill with Gizzy, who'd promised not to hurt me then pointed a fucking shotgun at me because his leader told him to."

A growl vibrates in my chest.

The bastard. The one person she opened herself to and he was a disloyal piece of shit. If I ever meet him, *I'll* kill him.

I place my hand on her trembling shoulder. "Ease up on the

gun, Anita, before your knuckles explode."

She slams the Glock into its holster. "Ow. *Dammit.*"

Tears glisten in her eyes. I resist the urge to gather her in my arms.

She's fully clothed but I still don't trust myself.

I take her hand, massaging my thumb into her palm. She hisses but doesn't swear at me.

"My own fault," she says. "Got what I deserved, believing in him. I won't make that mistake again."

"You can't let one arsehole stop you from trusting and finding someone who makes you happy."

"You think I should trust you?"

I grin, my fingers wrapped around her wrist. "Who better to trust than the guy pointing guns at you from the start?"

"At least you're honest about hating me."

"I don't hate you."

"You should."

Her eyes meet mine and dart away. My stomach clenches. She's been punishing herself better than I can.

She tugs on her arm. I tighten my grip and her breath catches. Her reaction to me… It drives me crazy.

"How about you believe I've forgiven you and I'll believe you trust me not to hurt you?"

I slide my hand up her arm, my thumb rubbing firm circles. She squirms under my fingers.

"Fine, okay, whatever. Can we go now?"

I brush the delicate skin at the bend of her elbow. She shivers and I press harder. Her nervousness sends excitement darting through my belly.

"Your pulse is racing."

She licks her lips. "I'm upset."

"Liar."

She jerks her arm free and cuddles it to her chest. "Lying is the only thing keeping me safe right now."

"From what, me?"

"No, from fucking aliens."

I grin. "You like me."

"Don't be ridiculous. You are unbelievably annoying."

"Baby, that's the truth."

Whoops. Probably shouldn't call her baby.

She blushes. "Are we done here? You got what you wanted."

"Not quite." I step closer. "Admit it."

Her laugh wobbles. "Admit what? You're delusional. Being alone out here has ruined your social skills."

"Always have to do things the hard way. Admit it and we can go."

"You said that already. Fine—I respect you, all right?"

"Try again."

I walk towards her. She scrambles backwards into a tree, staring at me like she's afraid I'll touch her.

And scared of how much she wants me to.

Or I'm projecting. I have to make sure.

"What are you doing?" she yelps, flinging up a hand. "I-I don't detest you."

"Getting warmer."

Her palm hits my chest, scorching over my heart. I trap it under my hand before she pulls away.

"Admit it."

"Why?"

"It's important to me."

"I admit nothing."

I roll my eyes. "God, you're stubborn."

"Damn right. Now let go or I'll hurt you."

"Oh, you won't hurt me."

Her eyes spark. She swings at me with her free hand. I catch her wrist beyond the bandage and hold both her hands to my chest, keeping my grip light.

She isn't pinned. She can still kick me in the nuts if she wants to.

"Okay, you win!" she squeaks, so different to her usual haughty tone. "I like you. Stupidly attracted. It's Stockholm syndrome. Or I'm a masochist. Pick your favourite."

Hello, sweet surrender.

"I knew I could make you talk."

She bares her teeth. "I hate you."

"No you don't."

I release her and heave the rucksack on. She sags against the tree and blinks at me.

"Why was that so important? What the hell do you want from me?"

"Confirmation."

"Why?"

Oh, you know why. "Guess we'll find out."

I leave her propped against the trunk, her pulse thudding in the hollow of her throat, her eyes dazed.

She's definitely into me.

<h1 style="text-align:center">23</h1>

"You don't want to get in the pod with me now?"

I laugh and Anita crosses her arms, her chin in the air. The flush on her cheekbones gives her away, obvious despite the dim interior of the abandoned farmhouse. Thick stone walls shelter us, the pod expanded on the dirt floor of the main room.

"You clearly can't be trusted, so no."

She has a point. I want that haughty voice to beg me to touch her. I can't do anything until she does and the restraint is agonising.

She seems more nervous around me now as a free woman than she ever did as my prisoner.

"I promise I will never do anything you don't want me to," I say, my voice serious in the darkening light.

It took us a while to reach a camping spot. The swinging death-trunk wasn't the only booby trap in the forest. We dodged tripwires, snares and pits of spikes, finally swapping the heavy gloom of trees and potential maiming for rank agricultural fields and chest-high weeds.

And the thought of what Anita might do.

She likes me. Despite my arsehole-ish tendencies and the faction I come from. Even more surprising—I like her. Despite... Well, you know. She's gotten under my skin, somehow. I can't decide whether I want to protect her or rip her clothes off.

Lie.

Both. Undeniably both.

She sidles towards the portal, never taking her eyes off me. I follow her tense shoulders inside, the awareness of me screaming in her muscles. She frowns at the floor and presses her wrists together, thrusting them under my nose.

"You asking me to tie you up?" I smirk and her gaze snaps to mine.

She splutters but rallies quickly. "You're not tying me up?"

"Would go against the whole forgiveness thing."

She ducks her head.

She doesn't believe me. I can't blame her. Everyone she trusted, everyone who should have supported her, hurt her. Why wouldn't I be the same? She destroyed my home and killed my brother.

I have more cause than any of them.

She gets ready for bed, removing her holster and placing it in easy reach, peeking at me as if I may snatch it back. She slips under the covers, staring at the ceiling as I slide in beside her. The heat of her settles against my skin, so close I could roll over and lose myself in it.

I turn on my side, my back to her, and listen to her breathing deepen.

Her body trusts me. Why else does she fall asleep so quickly? The rest of her will catch up. She'll soon forget about the twat-nozzle.

And all the other horrible things.

I shift, careful not to wake her.

The fading light of the pod glows on her skin. Sleep softens her face and relaxes her pouting mouth.

I remember the first time I saw her on Wick's video. The high cheekbones, the tumble of hair. Defiant and terrified. The sorrow and sickness I felt, knowing what was about to happen. The guilt at doing nothing as each new torture victim arrived and never left.

Thank god I had my brother.

Who did Anita have?

I don't want to be like everyone else. Their abuse scars her body and shadows her eyes.

I've glimpsed the person beneath the shields and the haughtiness. Playful, gentle, protective.

I want to see more of her.

24

I wake with Anita in my arms.

Huh. Guess I do cuddle her in my sleep.

Tension sings in her shoulders, her heartbeat quivering through her body but she lies still, her breathing even.

Pretending.

I roll away and prop myself up to look at her, a polite distance between us.

"Morning," I say.

What will it be this time—friendly greeting or straight to battle?

She licks her lips and jack-knifes into a sitting position. "Morning. We should get moving."

Ah, the old favourite of ignoring the problem completely.

She slides to the side of the pod and starts stuffing the covers into the rucksack. She pauses only long enough to fasten her Glock around her waist, her fingers lingering on the barrel.

"We should talk about what happened yesterday."

Her gaze flicks to me and away. "Nothing happened yesterday."

I should let her hide behind her stubbornness for a little longer but a flush rises in her cheeks, the dangerous glint in her eyes daring me to push her.

Not predator-prey but predator-predator.

Who will bleed first?

"You said you liked me."

"I was coerced." She jerks the sleeping bag from under my arse, and balls it into her lap.

"Okay, I'll give you that. How about we discuss what we're going to do now, then?"

"What are you, some kind of girl?" She pummels the air from a pillow and shoves it into the rucksack, leaving the one next to me.

"I know you're just lashing out because you're embarrassed, but that really hurts my feelings."

Her mouth twitches. She seems to catch herself and turns her laugh into a frown.

"I have nothing to be embarrassed about."

"You're right. You don't have to be embarrassed about liking me, Anita. I like you, too."

That sounded way cooler in my head.

"Fine," she says, clattering the cooking utensils together, "now we've established we're BFFs, are you ready to go?"

"Do you trust me not to hurt you?"

Her throat bobs. "There are lots of ways to hurt someone."

Liking me scares her. Or course it does. She was fooled by the twat-nozzle and he didn't have a dead brother to shove in her face.

"There are," I say softly, "and it sounds like you've experienced pretty much all of them. But I made you a promise."

"Great, because I don't want you to continue this conversation."

"I only want you to feel comfortable around me."

"I don't think that's ever going to be possible," she says on a sigh then shakes herself. "I mean, I think I'm as comfortable as I'm going to get. Good talk. Let's go."

She inches towards the portal, trailing the sleeping bag.

"Do you always run away from things you don't like?"

She glares at me. "I'm not running away."

I raise my eyebrow.

"Okay, you want to talk? Tell me about your first time in Wick's torture chamber."

I flinch. "What if I don't want to talk about that?"

I expect her to rage at me for being a hypocrite but her face pales and she hugs her knees to her chest.

"I'm sorry, forget I said it. You don't have to tell me anything. Some things are too terrible to share with anyone."

She didn't want to tell me her stuff and no wonder. Hers is all terrible.

"You shared your thing with me," I say.

"Again—I was coerced."

"Yeah, I really should stop doing that." I huff out a breath. "Guess it's only fair to tell you. I'll look bad if you're brave enough to talk about your thing but I'm not."

The colour returns to her face and she smirks. "Competitive, are we?"

"Oh, yeah. I like to win."

She can't hold my gaze, gathering the sleeping bag into her lap and fiddling with the material. A woman who can stare down would-be rapists in her underwear.

God, she is cute.

And I'm stalling. But she probably won't like me as much when I tell her about Wick.

How the hell did we get on this subject?

"The first time Wick ordered me into the torture chamber it

wasn't to be punished," I say, running my fingers through my hair. "He had a girl tied to the table. Naked. Terrified. She was just a kid."

I can still see her face: pretty, a sprinkling of freckles on pale cheeks, wide blue eyes.

I tried not to look at the rest.

"It's not your fault," Anita says. "Whatever he made you do, it's not your fault."

"Christ, I didn't think it'd be this hard. It was ages ago."

"But you've never told anyone?"

"Not even Dylan. I was embarrassed and just wanted to forget."

It was hard to forget when the risk of being ordered into the torture chamber increased each time I saw Wick. His black eyes always on me.

Would I have done what he said if he'd threatened to kill me? Put me on the table?

Probably.

I shiver. Anita stretches out on her back under the sleeping bag, holding the other side open.

So quick to offer comfort, even to me.

I lie down next to her, not touching.

"I'm worried you'll think less of me."

Yup, it does sound stupid out loud.

"Oh, come on. You heard my story—I turned into a shit-stained, quivering wreck. Plus, I already think you're an asshole, how much worse can it get?"

I manage a laugh. "True. It's easier knowing you've been in there. You know how terrifying it was. Nobody talked about it. We pretended it didn't happen. But you know."

"I know." Her hand finds mine beneath the covers and

squeezes tight.

Spit it out. Don't be a wimp.

"He wanted me to rape her," I say in a rush. "He thought it might be more damaging to be raped by someone who looked like me."

Personally, I think it'd be worse to be raped by someone with pitiless eyes and blood-encrusted fingernails but what do I know?

"I refused, obviously. Wick had three guards at that point: Selena, Christine and Doolly. They grabbed me. I fought them but you saw Doolly. They stripped me and dropped me on the girl. She screamed while they held me there, laughing, goading me on."

I can't tell if it's Anita's hand trembling, or my own.

"*I killed them*," she says. "Doolly and one of the Guard-bitches."

Her face is inches from mine, outrage sparking in her eyes. "Guard-bitches?"

"My name for Christine and Selena."

"We called them the Hell-twins. I would've killed them if they survived you but none of them did."

She shuts her eyes. I tug on her hand and she looks at me.

"You're thinking about Dylan."

"I'm sorry. I really am sorry."

"Wick is the reason my brother is dead. Of course you razed us after he brutalised you. He dragged us all down."

I was too stubborn to admit it. Too comfortable with my anger, the only thing keeping me alive in no man's land. Blaming Anita was easier than blaming myself and my whole screwed up faction.

"So I'm just going to say this next bit really fast to get it out of the way—they held me on top of the girl but I couldn't get an erection." I frown at the ceiling and manfully ignore the heat in my cheeks. "Wick was disappointed. Beat me with his rubber truncheon, but you can't make a guy get excited about raping someone. He injected me with a stimulant. Wasn't a normal needle. Went directly into the urethra."

Anita winces. I shudder and she grips my hand harder, the pressure helping to distract me from the humiliation.

"After twenty minutes, it had the desired effect, despite me never wanting to have sex again in my life. They tried to push me inside the girl but I struggled. She was hysterical. Wick acted as if it was hilarious but he told them to stop. I thought he'd kill me. Part of me didn't care. It'd hurt less." I don't mean to say so much but the words spill out. "The girl saw the goddamn erection and screamed some more. Wick handed me a knife. He said if I wouldn't rape her, I had two options: watch him with her or kill her myself."

"Jesus."

"She was just a kid, Anita. She looked at me and her face filled with hope. She wanted to live but she didn't understand what it meant. She had no idea what Wick would do to her."

But I knew. I'd seen it a few times already in shrieking, ripping, splattering detail.

"So I slid the knife into her heart," I say. "She didn't even flinch. I killed her because I couldn't stand to watch what Wick would do to her. I don't even regret it. I only wish I'd done it sooner. Not for her sake, but mine."

The simple truth makes me a selfish tool.

Anita shifts. I fix my gaze on the roof of the pod, avoiding her expression. The heat of her curls against me. I move my arm and she slots into my shoulder, her head on my chest. I force myself to keep breathing.

"She was dead as soon as Wick captured her," Anita says. "You let her go with minimal agony."

"Maybe. But what if she was like you? What if I'd left her alive and she managed to escape?"

"No one's like me."

I snort. "Truth."

Her fingertips stroke the tiny beads on the chains of my dog-tags through my t-shirt. A fine tremble jitters into my stomach.

Christ. I'm nervous. Why? I've already told her the worst of it.

And there's no one else in this world who understands what Wick could do better than her.

"What about your brother? Did Wick do the same to him?"

"Don't know. Thought about it, but I didn't want to know. He noticed I was distant. Never said anything. Wick either didn't approach him or he did and it didn't bother Dylan as much. I tried to forget and Wick left me alone. Apart from when I punched his guard in the face. God, I was petrified of what he'd do. When all he did was whip me, relief almost made it a reward. But it took me a while to let anyone close."

I really should have stopped talking a sentence ago.

"How did you? Let anyone close, I mean," Anita says.

I shrug, careful not to jostle her where she lies cuddled into me. "I got lonely."

Why do I always tell her everything?

"I imagine it didn't take long to find someone. I'm sure you had your pick of the ladies."

A laugh bubbles in my chest despite the recent subject matter, the awful words floating in the pod around us.

God, it feels good to let them out.

"You're not one for coddling, are you?" I say.

"I'd rather get you to laugh again than pat you on the head and say 'there, there.'"

Why does she care if I laugh?

"Are you not horrified, appalled, shocked?"

"All of those things. But for you, not by you."

I prop myself up instead of hugging her tight but can't resist tracing her cheek, her lips, my fingertips tingling.

"I'm glad I told you," I say.

"Me too."

She looks stunned somehow, but all I'm doing is smiling at her. I slide my hand into her hair, dazed by the feverish heat of her skin. She shifts closer, her face flushed, lips parted.

Holy crap, it's happening.

I keep my eyes on her and move slowly until her rapid breaths mix with mine.

"Do you trust me not to hurt you?" I say.

My heart beats far too loudly in the small space of silence.

If she says no, I'll never ask again.

"Yes," she whispers.

And finally—*finally!*—I kiss her.

25

It takes all my willpower not to devour Anita's mouth and drown in the taste.

I have to be gentle. I can't force her or claim what isn't mine (yet). It has to be perfect to chase the nervousness from her eyes.

So, no pressure.

She moans and fists her hand in my hair, her back arched, pressing her long, lithe body to mine. My self-control disintegrates. I thrust my hips into hers, my mouth bruising, desperate.

"Please, Blake. Please," she gasps.

Oh, you idiot.

I prop myself on trembling arms. "Tell me to stop, if that's what you want."

"God, no. Don't stop."

Thank you, Jesus. Now, show some restraint.

A tentative glide of lips teases her pouting mouth. She writhes underneath me, frantic noises in her throat. Our bodies shake to the throb of one swollen pulse.

And all we're doing is kissing.

"Please, please, please. We need to be naked." That haughty voice exactly as I wanted it—choked with desire, breathless, begging.

Freaking hell, I'm not going to last.

"Baby, you're killing me," I groan, collapsing on top of her, claiming her mouth before she can say anything else and drive me over the edge.

I unwrap her from her clothes and dodge her hands.

I have to keep my combats on as long as possible. I'll forget everything if she gets me naked.

I push myself up, drinking in the slender limbs, lean muscles and creamy skin framed by the wild tumble of her hair. Her cheeks are flushed, her lips half-parted. Green eyes stare back, as vulnerable as I've ever seen them.

I slide my fingers inside her. She cries out, bucking against my hand. My thumb circles her clitoris and one, long stroke is all it takes.

I grin. "So eager."

She blinks unfocused eyes at me.

Adorable.

"Oh, you bastard. Why did you have to be good?"

"You want me to be rubbish?"

I kiss along her jaw and down her neck, her pulse thundering under my lips. My hand skims her breast and her spine bows.

"No." The word sobs, frustrated and needy.

Man, her responsiveness…Just awesome.

My tongue follows her collarbone.

I plan on heading straight to orgasm number two. Three in total seems a good number for her first time with me.

She unfastens my combats and curls her slim fingers around my erection.

Nope. I can't wait any longer.

Number two will have to be spectacular.

I kick out of my trousers and force myself to take one last look at her, naked and open and willing underneath me.

"Blake, please. I need you. Inside me."

I swallow a growl, fighting the unbearable need to thrust myself deep. I lower myself to a whisper away from her.

"Finally," I say against her lips, "she speaks the truth."

She pulls me into her searing heat and matches me, all soft and silk and steel.

God, the feel of her, the way she moves…

My whole body aches, the pressure building in my balls, my shaft, hell, even my toes. I try to hold on, focus on something except the slide of her skin and the dance of her hips and the delicious friction somehow tingling through every part of me and not just the bit buried inside her. A whimper sticks in her throat, her muscles tightening around me. I practically explode, my cries joining hers and echoing in my ears.

Sweet-holy-fricking-hell.

Please tell me I didn't say that out loud.

Maybe after two months, any sex would've felt amazing. I should wait for the endorphins to fade before I ask her to marry me.

I reassemble myself, panting into her neck, her heart competing with mine for whose can beat the loudest. Her arms wrap around me, her fingertips trailing over my shoulders to stroke my scars. I shiver and lift my head. Satisfaction curls in my gut at the sated glow of her skin, the swollen lips and tousled hair. I brush it out of her face and kiss her.

Still light, delicate.

"What have you done to me, you wicked temptress?" I say.

She laughs, her muscles tensing in intimate areas and driving me mad.

Maybe we can reach number three after all.

She cocks her eyebrow. "Already?"

Doubting my stamina. That won't do.

I smile. Slow, wicked. "I like to win."

I rotate my hips and she moans, her eyelids fluttering.

"What have you won?" she says, struggling to look at me.

No fear, no panic.

"You," I whisper.

26

The change in Anita is incredible. She's affectionate, the wariness gone. All I have to do is touch her and it melts her steely control. She can't keep her hands off me.

Me and my magic penis.

She tries to hide behind a not-so-subtle grilling on my background as we break camp and head towards the east coast.

Her plan to escape the country now sounds like a brilliant idea. My one caveat is a change to the destination. We'll be lucky if anything is left in Eyemouth harbour but we can find vessels further north.

Unification Army moors warships from their stronghold in Dunbar in a bay when on patrol.

Sometimes Wick gleaned useful information from his victims. Mostly, he preferred their screams.

Overgrown agricultural fields continue in an endless patchwork broken by trees and tangled hedgerows, heat waves shimmering over all of it.

"What was your role in Livingston or did you just work on the dragon?"

I hide a smile at question number one hundred and twenty, or thereabouts.

Is she trying to absolve herself, mask the embarrassment, or is she so smitten she wants to know everything about me?

My ego favours the latter.

"The dragon took up a chunk of time but I managed the jets when not working on her. Advanced to team leader. Dylan was jealous of that one. I officially got to boss him around, though didn't do it for that. I was making myself invaluable so Wick wouldn't drag me back into the torture chamber."

Bitterness fills her laugh. "I thought I was pretty invaluable. Respected. Turns out Marshall just viewed me as another Carmichael to fuck and be conquered."

"Don't take this the wrong way, I absolutely hate the guy—he's a vile sexual predator—but a tiny bit of me understands his obsession." I grin and sidle out of reach, recognising the glint in her eyes.

She follows me across a ditch on the edge of a field. "What, I lure men with my aura of charm and mystery?"

"I'm here, aren't I?"

"I have no idea why you're here. With me."

"You think I should've killed you? Hurt you and abandoned you with nothing?"

"It's what I did to you. What I deserve."

I shake my head. "Everything you said when we first met was true—it's a war, people die; I'd have done the same—but I didn't want to listen."

"I killed your brother."

Each mention hurts a little less. "You didn't personally look him in the eye and bash his head in. You had no idea who or where he was. You were a force of nature. A vengeful bitch of one but a force of nature nonetheless."

"The bitch part is right."

We skirt an impenetrable field of brambles. Heat shimmers

above the few bare patches of dirt.

"Seems like you've been punishing yourself better than I have," I say. "Maybe we deserve a little happiness. You've lost someone, too."

"But you didn't kill my sister."

"That was unfair of me to say."

"No, it wasn't."

"Do you always argue, even when it's in your favour?"

The scowl on her face says yes, yes she does.

Trees finally shade us from the sun's glare and the unending fields. A river burbles somewhere in the gloom, the scent of loam and pine rich on the air.

"Anyway, what's with the background check? You deciding if I'm trustworthy?"

A delicate pink flushes her cheeks. "Sorry."

So easy. So cute. She blushes so frequently, I'm surprised she has blood elsewhere in her body.

I cup her face. "You're sexier when you blush."

The blush flares and I can't resist kissing her. Her arms wrap around my waist, pulling me against her. I let myself kiss her harder despite the heightened risk of wanting to slam her to the ground and take her like an animal.

Tongues and teeth.

Anita moans into my mouth, her fingers gripping my arse, her hips grinding into my erection.

I pull away instead of ripping her clothes off. "God, woman. You make it easy to forget where we are. But this does seem as good a place as any to set up camp."

A grassy hollow opens beside the river, sheltered by a cliff of earth, trees and dangling roots. The water has carved a trench, swirling into a lazy pool beneath a rock face.

Anita sets up camp, darting glances at me. Her shyness stirs excitement in my chest. I corner her in the pod and press her to the newly smoothed covers, slipping my hands under her t-shirt to play across her ribs. I swallow her small pleasure sounds, each one firing to my groin.

We need to be naked.

I pull her t-shirt off and kiss down her neck to the slickness of the bullet scar at her shoulder. I tease it with my tongue and she jumps, her breath shuddering out. I fist my hand in the covers.

She's the only woman who can shatter my control.

I move to the abdominal scar, a ridge of tissue separating the taut planes of her stomach.

It doesn't ruin her perfection. It's part of her and a reminder to me.

My mouth explores it and she trembles under my touch.

"When did you get this?"

Her throat works, her eyes already half-dazed. "In Calders. Before I stole the dragon."

"What did you lose?"

"Spleen and part of my liver."

"You don't have knife scars. Well, not recent ones."

I stroke my fingertips across her stomach, tracing a tiny silvery line near her hip. There are a couple more.

Another person who attacked her. She survived but what toll does it take when everyone—even her own faction and people she allowed herself to be intimate with—tries to kill her? We all live under death's shadow but there's always some reprieve. Bursts of light in the dark.

"I was beaten. After I was shot."

The desire in her voice boosts my ego immensely, considering the topic of conversation. She seems more distracted by the teasing caress of my fingers.

Baby, it's about to get a million times better.

"And you flew to Fellhill in the dragon like that?"

"I'm a stubborn bitch."

"Yeah you are." Pride heats the words and I speak the rest without thinking. "I won't let anyone hurt you again."

She closes her eyes. I stop myself from scooping her into my arms.

"You don't believe me? That's okay, I'll prove it to you." I kiss the skin above the waistband of her combats, curling my fingers under the material. "What's the opposite of pain? Oh, yes."

I lick where my lips were and her eyes snap open. Wide, panicked. Smirking, I unfasten her trousers and slide them down her hips.

"Wait!"

"Why?"

She seems to have trouble focusing. "I don't know."

"God, you're still fighting your attraction to me. That is so fucking sexy."

Her love of swearing has rubbed off on me.

The underwear follows her combats, tossed to the side of the pod. She fists her right hand in the covers, biting her lip and watching me. I give her a wicked smile and spread her legs.

I have to take a moment just to look at her. Eyelids fluttering, the rapid rise and fall of her chest. Naked and vulnerable and eager for me to touch her. I wriggle onto my belly and nibble the inside of her thigh, her skin silky and warm. She moans, her spine bowed.

Christ, she makes me so hard, it's painful.

She blinks lovely, dazzled eyes at me. "Blake, please."

My clothes suffocate me. My skin is burning, aching, yearning to be pressed to hers and buried in her warmth.

Must keep clothes on.

A few deep breaths reduce the risk of me coming in my pants at the sight of her arousal. It also gets me wondering what else she might tell me. She finally admitted to liking me out in the death-trap woods. What more will she reveal when denied release and teased to the brink of sanity?

Okay… More deep breathing.

"What's your biggest fear?" I say.

Something flashes across her face but she smothers it.

"Spiders," she gasps. "I'm deathly afraid of spiders."

She has to do it the hard way.

I chuckle and place a soft kiss between her legs. "Liar. Try again."

She writhes on the twisted covers. I lower my head and she tenses. Swallowing a groan, I nibble her other thigh and tickle the backs of her knees, massaging up the quivering muscles of her legs. The heat of her stuns my senses.

"That's not fair. I can't think… Blake."

I love my name on her lips. Especially when it shakes. Breathy and begging. She has no idea the glorious denial is as excruciating for me as it is for her.

"Tell me."

"Being alone. And you."

I manage to control my expression but speaking takes a couple of attempts. "You're afraid of me? You weren't afraid when I was marching you around at gunpoint but now you're scared?"

"Yes."

"Why?"

She shakes her head, her hair falling across her face. I lick her and almost lose myself in the taste. She jerks upright. I force myself to stop and she slumps into the pillows.

"You bastard," she says, her eyes half-lidded.

"Tell me something I don't know."

"Marching me around at gunpoint made sense. But this, this I don't understand."

"What's to understand? When we met in the woods, I was close to giving up. Exhausted, starving. I had nothing but grief. You had what I needed and I took it. Felt justified knowing you were The People's Republic. Discovering you were the one—Wick's last prisoner—I wanted to hurt you. But you were not what I expected. You've been hurt worse by so many people. What right did I have to punish you for something you couldn't control?"

Her trembling transfers to me through my grip on her thighs, her pulse thudding under my fingers.

"I could've flown away. Killed Wick and left the rest of you."

"Really? Thinking we were sadists like him? Wondering if we'd watch the video of your ordeal? Knowing we would attack Calders to take back what was ours?"

She shudders. "No, okay? I had to. I had to destroy you so I could live. Heal. Forget. I'm sorry."

"You don't need to apologise anymore. I'm the one who's sorry. But I'll make it up to you."

I skim my fingers higher over the fascinating jut of her hipbones to her taut stomach. Her heels dig into the floor, arching her hips but my weight on her thighs pins her.

I lower my head. "You still scared?"

"Terrified," she pants.

"Baby, I guess you'll have to trust me."

I press my mouth between her legs and kiss her properly. She squirms, her breath sobbing out, each moan pulsing through my body. I let myself explore, linger. Suck and lick each fold and drown in the honeyed taste of her.

"Oh god, oh god, oh god," she whispers, over and over.

I have the feeling I won't get cramp with her.

Pressure builds in my groin as if I may just come right alongside her.

This has never happened before. Sure, pleasuring women turns me on but not to the brink of orgasm.

I struggle to control the rising tension, my heartbeat roaring in my ears and throbbing in my cock. Anita's mewling gasps don't help, her body arched and trembling above me. Hot and aching and ready to fall.

Jesus god, *focus!*

I concentrate on spelling my name across her clitoris with my tongue.

Mine. Mine, now.

She stops breathing, quivering on the edge. I fasten my mouth on her and suck, slipping my tongue inside her. Her sharp cry echoes around the pod and her muscles clench around me. I force myself to keep still while she writhes, the risk of exploding in my trousers embarrassingly close. She collapses into the covers, her legs splayed, body limp, sweat dewing her skin. I chuckle against her and she yelps. I scoop her into my arms and cuddle her to my chest.

"Not alone anymore," I say.

I desperately need to learn how to shut myself up.

27

Fighting the overwhelming need to bury myself inside Anita nearly kills me. But if I do, one stroke and I'll be done.

She deserves at least another orgasm, though I'm beginning to doubt my self-control.

Cold water helps.

I carry her into the river, her head lolling on my shoulder.

No questions, no sass. She seems to have lost the power of speech.

Satisfaction burns in my chest, smothering the iciness of the water climbing my thighs.

She shivers and I hold her tighter. "Don't worry, I'll warm you up soon."

Her breath catches.

Just awesome.

Water swirls over my waist, cooling the dangerous heat. Anita hisses and wriggles higher. I shift her so her legs wrap around my waist and I stare into startled eyes of green and gold and bronze.

I press her back to the rock face. "Now, I'm going to fuck you. Hard."

"Yes, please," she gasps, no hesitation.

She doesn't beg, not for anyone. Except me.

A rush of tenderness weakens my knees, the fierceness unexpected.

Who knew I was such a girl?

I grip her thighs and angle her hips. I thrust inside her, surrendering to the reckless desire I suppressed when she hugged me in her underwear and drove all sense from my brain.

She takes me in, pulls me closer, her hips matching mine. I capture her mouth and swallow her moans. I press her hands to the stone, our fingers entwined. She arches against me and I fill her velvet heat.

"God, Anita, you are freaking amazing," I groan.

Silky muscles tense around me. My breath rushes out. Her soft cries dance on the surface of the water. The pressure tightens my balls and threatens to burst me apart. Her head flops to the side, her eyes half-lidded. I stop—a delicious, agonising pause—and her eyes snap open.

"Look at me," I growl. "I want to see your face when I make you come."

"Blake, oh god, don't stop. Please don't stop."

How can I refuse?

I drive myself into her, captivated by the flushed skin and drowning eyes, her pupils dilated, the remaining iris darkening to emerald. The trust there stuns me. I can't hold on any longer. The glorious tension surges, tearing a cry from my throat. I pulse inside her, as deep as I can go. She bucks against the rock wall, her cries joining mine. I collapse into her and everything goes a little hazy apart from the thunder of her heart answering the thud of my own.

* * *

A naked woman is straddling me.

Best wake-up call ever.

Anita kisses the corner of my mouth. "Morning."

Before I can reply, her lips find mine. Demanding, taking. I open to the slide of her tongue, my heart leaping under the press of her body. I flex my hips, my hands pulling her tighter against me, rubbing my erection into the slickness, oh so close.

She gasps and breaks the kiss. I blink at her, trying to restart my brain. Her mouth trails down my neck and scalds along my collarbone, her tongue lapping the hollow of my throat. I shudder and she slides lower, licking my nipple, each soft stroke jittering to my stomach. A feeling close to panic expands in my chest. She moves lower still, sucking on my stomach, her hot breath caressing my straining cock.

Oh god, she's going to—

"Anita, wait. I haven't—I won't—"

She licks me and banishes my ability to speak. Her mouth sears every nerve, enfolding me in its heat.

Goodbye, self-control.

My own fault. Most women are happy to take without giving if you don't make a big deal about it.

When I finally open my eyes, Anita smirks at me. "Now who's the eager one?"

My face warms.

Maybe she won't notice.

I clamp my legs around her waist and roll her over.

"You're going to regret that," I whisper into her throat.

She swallows, her pulse jumping against my lips. "I regret nothing. About time you lost control. I can't be the only slavering idiot around here."

I kiss her collarbone, sliding one hand across her ribs to her breast. She moans, already squirming.

"No deal. It's more fun when it's you. And it's not my fault—you caught me off-guard."

"Off-guard? I barely had to touch you."

The cheek of her.

I flex my hips and she arches into me.

I chuckle. "Oh no, you're not getting that yet, you wanton little hussy."

I fight temptation and lift myself off. She pouts. I manage not to bite her.

"That's not fair. At least I didn't demand to hear your secrets."

I move onto my back and pull her into me, cuddling her to my side. A wandering hand slides down my stomach but I capture it and place it on my chest.

"You want secrets? Okay then. I haven't been touched like that in a while."

She stops trying to tug her hand free and raises her head. "I guess two months would seem like an eternity for someone like you."

"What's that supposed to mean?"

"Oh, come on. You scream sex. Your eyes, your body. It all says, 'I am awesome in bed. You will beg for me.'"

I bite my lip to muffle a happy noise. "Awesome, am I?"

"I... Shut up."

"And you're what, sexless? Have you looked in a mirror?"

"Fine, fine. I'm easy on the eyes. Most men just see the blonde hair."

"While I'll admit it is a distraction, it's not what I see."

The eyes. A beautiful green changing with her expression, be it furious, defiant or—as I've recently discovered—tender. Trusting.

Don't screw it up.

"You also a tits and ass man?"

Surprised, I laugh. "Don't remind me. I'm glad you shot the sneering twat. I wanted to kill him for touching you."

"You hadn't touched me then."

"The scars finally made me notice how often you've been hurt. I wanted to protect you."

"That's not all you wanted."

I avoid her gaze. "God, I was pissed at myself. Pawing at you. After what the guy might have done."

"My reaction was hardly revulsion."

"I can never tell with you." I slide my fingers through her hair to cup her head. "You're not like any other enemy I've met."

Or any other woman.

"And that's why you wanted confirmation?"

"Confirmation it definitely wouldn't be rape."

She smiles softly and kisses me. I pull her closer, one hand still buried in her hair. Freed, she strokes her fingers downward, tickling my stomach. I catch her hand and press it over my heart.

"Now you're the one who can't keep her hands to herself."

She drops her eyes. "Well, that wasn't much of a secret. Of course you haven't met another woman out here. None you'd touch without gloves and some strong bleach, anyway."

"I wasn't finished. You diverted me by saying how awesome I am."

The delicate flush spreads. "Go on then. Finish it."

"It was longer than two months."

"You said you were all having lots of sex in Livingston."

Am I really telling her this?

"Sex, yes, but… I focused on them having a great time. Didn't force them to reciprocate. I still got intercourse."

It started after Wick, when I finally let myself get close to someone. I needed to know they damn well wanted to be there and I built a reputation for generosity. Others came to expect it. Sure, I missed being on the receiving end but shied away from anything involving coercion. Though it grated that no one took the initiative because they wanted *me* to feel good.

"The women of Nationless are idiots. How could they not touch you like that?"

Seriously, can Anita read my mind?

I struggle to appear nonchalant. "Most people are selfish. But not you. You look at me like…"

Her throat bobs, a hint of panic on her face. "Like what?"

"Like you see me. Know me. Like… I don't know. Something deeper."

Great, eloquent. I'm not out to hurt her anymore but I still have no idea what I'm doing.

"Oh, I see you all right. I'm going to have such fun with you." Her mouth hovers over mine. "I'm due some payback."

Breathe. Speak. Act like a big, tough man instead of a squirmy little virgin.

"Payback for what?"

"For turning me into a slavering idiot."

She smirks, a knowing, sexy smirk. My signature move turned against me. Part of me is impressed. The rest feels like a lightning bolt has struck between my eyes and sizzled down every nerve in my body.

Her lips glide over mine, tormenting me. She pulls away and I can't stop a whimper. She makes her own eager noise low in her throat and melts into me. Her heart thrums against my hand linked with hers and trapped between us. I ache to slide her into my lap and have her above me, riding me, watching me with those—

I roll, breaking the kiss, somewhat breathless. "Dammit, woman. I was the one getting payback. How do you do that?"

She blinks at me and I chuckle.

"Okay, the expression on your face is worth it. If you behave yourself, maybe I'll get you to moan my name later."

"Blake…"

"Mmm. Like that but a bit *breathier*."

While she splutters, I clamber away from the temptation of her and dig clothes from the rucksack.

"What are you doing?" she says.

"Come on, get dressed. Let's go hunting."

"Hunting?"

Such pouting disappointment.

"God, woman, do you only think of one thing? We're low on food. If you want to keep humping like rabbits, we need sustenance."

Her lovely blush, absent for mere minutes, returns to paint her cheeks and warm my chest. The glow increases as she tugs on combats and a t-shirt without glancing at them. She frowns at me and drops her gaze.

"Oh, goddammit," she sighs.

My smirk widens.

I have to admit, my navy t-shirt and trousers look better on her.

"Always wearing my clothes. If you want to be my girlfriend, you just have to ask."

Girlfriend? Where did that come from?

"Shut up," she growls, and flees.

28

Thunder scares the deer and ruins my shot, otherwise I definitely would've hit it. Instead of bagging a juicy hunk of venison, the blue-white bolt from the electrigun strikes a birch and crisps the bark.

"Shit," I sigh.

Anita is a bad influence on my vocabulary.

She muffles a snort behind me.

"You better not be laughing at me, woman."

She shakes her head, a hand clamped over her mouth, her eyes dancing. I step towards her and try to look menacing.

"You—set fire to—a tree," she gasps. "Such skill."

"What did I say about behaving?"

"You're right, you're right. A feast of charred bark awaits."

Oh, that mouth.

I lunge for her but she dodges with a yelp and sprints through the trees, her laughter wild. The excitement of the chase throbs in my blood, urging me to run her down and sink my teeth—or, more likely, another part of my anatomy—into her. She traps herself in a bramble patch, spinning on the spot, searching for a way out. I curl my fingers into fists to keep from burying them in her hair and dragging her against me. She darts out of reach, her squeal inciting the thrill shivering through my stomach. With a burst of speed, I tackle her to the ground, pin her hands above her head and straddle her hips.

"You're not perfect," she says, her chest heaving. "Hallelujah!"

The shivers spread upwards. "You think I'm perfect?"

"Not anymore," she sniggers, wriggling underneath me. "Oh, god. Stomach hurts. Not laughed—so much—in ages."

"It's only been a few days. Lobbing fish at me amused you."

"Don't remind me. Hilarious. Your *face*."

And hers. Laughter-bright, flushed, eyes sparkling. Playful, even then.

A glimpse of the person she could be if I was strong enough to forgive her.

"God, you're beautiful," I whisper.

Must stop saying everything out loud.

I kiss her to shut myself up. Her fingers tighten in mine, her mouth opening to me. Thunder rumbles, quieter than the pulse roaring in my ears, the charged air difficult to breathe.

I push myself up. "I like hearing you laugh."

What did I just say?!

"Not had much to laugh about before now."

That can be goal number two: always make her laugh. Goal number one is, obviously, give her as many orgasms as physically possible.

Lightning flickers, captured in her pupils and daring me to follow.

Can you lose yourself in someone's eyes?

The ground tilts, a sensation like falling. She looks away.

I shake myself. "Me neither. Even with Dylan, Livingston wasn't a happy place. Wick's damn torture videos."

Anita quivers, the approaching storm darkening the woods and shadowing her face. A drop of rain strikes her cheek and trickles down.

I stand and hold out a hand. "Come on. Before we get soaked."

We run through the trees. A wall of hissing rain dogs our steps. I aim for a shallow overhang of rock, roots dangling over the entrance. A tug on my hand slows me down and Anita darts ahead. Drops speckle my t-shirt. I trail her into the coolness of the shelter and fist my hand in her hair, pulling her against me. Her eyes glint a challenge.

"Just because I've decided you can live doesn't mean you get to stop being placatory."

She smirks. "At least you're not a hard man to please."

"That mouth of yours. It must have gotten you into so much trouble."

"You have no idea."

I have some idea, though it seems to be getting me into more trouble than her these days.

I close the tiny distance between us and capture her lips, forcing myself to be gentle despite my grip in her hair.

Teasing produces the best reactions.

She moulds herself to me, her fingers tight on my waist. Her eager noises threaten to fracture my control. Her hips grind into mine and I ease her away. She blinks at me, trembling in my hands.

"Could you ever refuse me?"

She thrusts her chin in the air. "Yes. If I wanted to."

"Liar."

"You don't have to be so smug."

"Sure I do. This definitely means I win."

"We'll see. I'm not finished with you yet."

I sling my arm around her shoulders. "I hope not."

Rain drums the soil and batters the leaves. Water cascades from the overhang and separates us from the world. The shushing roar fills me with a peaceful lethargy, the warmth of Anita at my side.

"You want to hear another secret?" I say almost lazily.

"What?"

I told her the worst one, this is nothing. Well, maybe not nothing…

"Wick was attracted to me."

Her gaze zips to mine, her eyes wide. "He what?"

"After he whipped me—when I was stripped to the waist, my hands bound above my head, bleeding—he said if he liked guys, he'd spend every day buried inside me."

She shudders. "Sweet-fucking-Jesus. Why does that make me think of him ripping you open rather than something tender and intimate?"

"Because you met him."

Lightning blazes into our shelter, flaring monochrome.

"I'm sorry you had to live with him. I barely managed five days but you survived *years*. He tortured you in his own way. Did Dylan know?"

I shake my head. "Couldn't tell him. You're the only one who knows all my secrets."

Her eyes shimmer but lightning flashes and it's gone.

"Thank you," she whispers.

I hug her tighter. "It gets worse."

"Of course it does."

"He forced me to watch while he called in one of his women to service him. Janine. I don't know how she stomached it. Everything he did and she worshipped him."

"I knew Janine—dark hair, pixie features?"

"Yeah. How?"

"From before. We worked together. We were friends. She was nothing like I remember."

"Are you saying you haven't changed? You've always been this warrior-woman who can't form more than two sentences without using the f-word?" I manage a smile.

"Okay, so there may have been less swearing. And some girlish softness."

"Can't picture it."

"Don't you mock me."

"Or what? You'll hurt me with your girlish softness?"

Her wicked grin sucks the air from my chest.

I tense. "Don't—"

She ducks under my arm, and shoves. I stumble into the battering rain, and dripping roots slap me in the face. Warm water plasters my clothes to my body in seconds.

"How's that for soft?" comes the laughing response from the dryness of the overhang.

I whirl, my own wicked smile on my lips. Startled eyes peek from behind the flimsy barrier. I lunge through the waterfall spilling from the top of the cliff-face and wrap my fingers around her wrist.

"Wait!" she squeaks.

"Oh, I don't think so."

I tug her into the rain. She trips and I catch her, my arms circling her slim waist, her hands on my shoulders.

"It's actually quite refreshing."

She cups my face, her thumb tracing my bottom lip. "You're beautiful, too."

I suddenly find it harder to breathe.

She watches me like—like she...

Don't be a moron.

I swallow. "Beautiful, awesome and nearly perfect? You're going to turn me into a narcissist."

Her fingers tickle along my collarbone and dip into the hollow of my throat.

Can she feel my pulse racing?

Her eyes darken and my heart kicks.

A growl rumbles in my chest. "God, I love the way you look at me."

I lift her up and her legs wrap around my hips. Her mouth claims mine, slippery with water.

I want to lick every drop from her body. I love how she tastes. Cherry and almonds. I love how she can't say no to me, a gentle touch all it takes to awaken her desire. I love—

That's plenty.

I drop to my knees and press her to the ground, mud oozing over my splayed hands.

She doesn't need to know it's because I've lost the strength to stand.

She arches underneath me, peeling my sodden t-shirt off. My dog-tags swing and she catches them in her fist.

Her expression is naked, trusting, tender, as though she's cradling my heart.

It rips me open.

I bury myself in her and she screams my name into the storm. *Mine.*

29

Anita has fun with me the next morning, too. She also has talented hands. No, not talented.

Bloody amazing.

I last a little longer but not by much. From iron self-control to ejaculating like a teenager. Kinda embarrassing.

But worth the delight on her face.

We break camp, my legs still wobbling, and she shoulders the rucksack. We follow the river east, the air cool under the trees but threatening to melt our faces off on leaving the shade.

"Blake?" She frowns at the sun-dappled ground, her hands curled around the straps of the rucksack, the bandage on her arm flashing white.

It's so easy to forget she's injured. She hides it well. No weakness.

"Yeah?"

"I think I'll use both my mouth and hands on you later." Wicked, wicked smile. "Bet I can break my record."

I stumble into a bush, the branches snapping under my boots. "Woman, are you trying to kill me?"

She smirks and darts ahead despite the heavy rucksack.

She also makes it easy to forget the danger we're in, abandoning the Borderlands for Unification Army territory. Each step takes us closer to an unknown future somehow more terrifying than my two months in no man's land.

I mean, what the hell am I going to do with Anita, introduce her to my mother?

The woodland ends in a wash of blistering sunlight, shimmering fields stretching to the horizon. I follow Anita into the whispering grass, one hand on my gun.

I fell asleep cuddling her, her face in my neck, her soft breath teasing my pulse. The storm confined us to the pod after we staggered back. We talked in hushed voices as the opal light faded.

She said John Anders gave her the first silvery scars and I hated him more. She told me how her friends betrayed her, how Marshall used it to his advantage. How the bastard was the one who murdered her sister and started this mess.

He turned Wick into a monster.

Every new insight increased the crazy protectiveness burning a hole in my chest.

Best to ignore it. She may watch me like I'm wonderful but, for her, it's just sex. Mind-blowing but sex all the same. It doesn't matter how I feel, she'll move on eventually.

I've seen it a million times.

Except with Rachael. She was shy. Sweet. She wanted to wait a little before we slept together (not that I admitted it to Dylan when he asked). Maybe we could've been something special.

If not for Anita.

Sunlight gilds her hair, the golden tumble parted around the rucksack and falling over her shoulders. A green t-shirt and combats hug her chest and legs. She glides through the weeds, her gait a stalking sway of hips, a Glock at her waist.

Beautiful and deadly.

My cock twitches.

I could stride up to her, spin her around and crush my mouth to hers. She won't refuse me. I could slam her into the dust, grass awns in her hair, and she'll moan my name. No games. I could sink into her and forget everything but the taste of her skin. I—

Jesus, would you stop it!

This is an enjoyable interlude, a way to heal. *For both of us.* If we reach the outside world and it's whatever passes for normal these days, she'll go find her parents and I'll head to Ireland, never to see each other again.

This isn't some fairy tale.

The fields spit us onto the remains of a motorway, the surface cracked and covered in soil.

"Christ, look at that," Anita says, walking further up the road. "I guess the rest of the world tried to respond after all."

Twisted vehicles sit on the concrete, their organisation logos almost lost beneath the soot and bullet holes. Craters shatter the motorway, weeds peeking through.

Welcome to Scotland.

We dart across the central reservation and climb an embankment to the ruin of a railway line that droops wires and rust. A dirt track leads uphill on the other side, flanked by trees and overgrown fields.

Anita halts at the top amidst crumbling buildings and broken stone. "Stay and rest a minute. Christ, it's hot."

"Never would have pegged you as unfit."

"I can see you gasping and sweating from here. You're not even wearing the rucksack."

I pretend to scratch my chin on my shoulder instead of

wiping my face. "I'm not sweating, I'm glowing."

"Of course. My bad."

God, I can't get enough of her mouth.

The growl of engines somewhere on the other side of the woodland ruins the moment. Anita's eyes meet mine.

"Well, that can't be good," I say.

She drinks a mouthful of water from our bottle and passes it to me. "Hide or keep moving?"

The engines sputter and die.

"Hide. Less noisy."

We hustle into the ruins of a village, crouching in a building with three walls left standing. Anita peers through a broken window facing the road, sunlight winking off the splinters of glass left in the frame.

"Reminds me of the day I met you," she says.

I brace my shoulder on the other side of the window. "How so?"

"I heard an engine that time, too. Hid in a tree while four guys searched for me. Borderlanders, I think. One of them stepped on a mine."

"I heard it from my own hideout in a tree." I remember her hurrying through the forest, beautiful and tense. "You escaped them to get jumped by me."

"Not a great day but not one of my worst. Seeing where it actually led, I guess it became one of my best."

I smile at her and hope it isn't too soppy.

She always says the perfect thing to unman me.

Her gaze drops to my mouth, her green eyes filling with the hunger that tingles through my cock and drives me crazy, even now.

"This is hardly the time, woman," I say, scrabbling to hold

onto my frayed willpower.

She blushes and frowns out the window.

Amazing.

We wait half an hour but nothing stirs in the woods. We creep from our hiding place and stick to the forest before rejoining the road. The path stretches empty in both directions.

"Maybe they weren't looking for us." The wind dances Anita's hair across her face, her Glock still in her hand.

"Maybe. Seems like too much of a coincidence, though. In my experience, people don't wander around in no man's land without a compelling reason."

My reason—no encampment left to live in. Hers—betrayal and pain, the dangerous wilds safer than staying with the twat-nozzle.

And all the other arseholes who'd hurt her.

"That's what I thought, too, but it's getting pretty crowded out here."

We walk and scan the forest on either side of the road, our weapons ready. Something flits through the trees beside me. Shifting patches of green and black.

Oh, fu—

The crack of a gunshot vibrates in my chest, loud enough to fracture my ribs. A bullet puffs into the dirt.

"Move, and the next goes into someone's skull," a voice says.

30

Dylan would've looked dainty next to the four men who emerge from the forest, two on either side of the track. Combat paint darkens their skin, their SA80 rifles tight against camouflage-patterned uniforms.

"Ladykiller, get their weapons," the soldier on the right barks, flicking his rifle towards us. "Both of you drop your guns or things get messy."

Ladykiller? The name is nearly as stupid as Gizzy the twat-nozzle.

With two rifles pointed at my chest, I do what the soldier says. Anita's Glock thumps into the dirt in tandem to my Browning. A bald man on the far left of the line of muscle steps forward. He grins, sidling over to me, his eyes on Anita. I itch to lift my arm and zap his face.

"Ladykiller?" Anita raises her eyebrow in her best haughty expression.

The man's shit-eating grin widens. "You'll find out why soon enough."

Not while I'm breathing.

He stops level with my shoulder, shoving the barrel of his gun into my temple. I grit my teeth to keep from punching him.

"Remove that contraption from your arm. Toss it over there."

The electrigun hits the dirt between us and the rest of the he-men. Ladykiller disappears behind me, one meaty hand patting me down, taking my two knives and swiping my gun from the ground.

"On your knees, hands on your head."

Great, defenceless and on my knees again. I have the feeling these guys won't be as easy to kill as the Borderlanders.

Which means we're dead.

"Please," Anita whispers, her eyes wide, "don't hurt him. We'll do what you want."

Low and trembling voice.

Is she faking it? Hoping to trick them into believing she isn't a threat?

Good idea. The man who seems to be in charge is already preoccupied by her breasts.

I want to pluck out his eyeballs.

"Don't worry, it's you we're after. We don't have many women in our encampment." He manages to switch his gaze to her face. "None that look like you, anyhow."

And it's going to stay that way, jackass.

Ladykiller tugs the rucksack from Anita's back, hard enough to make her stumble. He claims her Glock, knife and the unfamiliar handgun. She doesn't struggle, her spine straight and stiff, her face pale.

Unarmed and vulnerable.

Ladykiller returns to my side, propping the rucksack at his feet. "What now, Bossman?"

Bossman? Are you serious?

"Kill him."

"No!"

The desperate cry slaps the trees and a weight slams me onto my back. My breath huffs out, my face pressed to the warmth of a body above me.

Cherries and almonds and a heartbeat thudding against my cheek.

Anita curls around me, her arms and legs gripping mine. A hiss shivers in her chest. She shifts, flashes of boots and dirt visible through the fall of her hair.

"We want you alive but we don't need you whole," Bossman says, his voice close. "Move or we will hurt you and kill him slowly."

Neither option sounds good to me.

"Please," she gasps, shaking, holding me tighter. "I'll come with you. I won't fight. Just don't kill him. *Please.*"

Thank Christ her body hides my face. I can't control my expression.

She doesn't beg but pleading for my life appears to be another exception.

Her weight disappears to leave me gaping at the sky. I shiver despite the heat. Anita thrashes between the two remaining soldiers, their fingers smearing paint on her arms. Her hair is mussed around her face, her chest heaving. Tears well in eyes raw with pain.

Not faking.

She cares about me. The guy who tried to kill her, marched her around at gunpoint and berated her. Last survivor of a faction she hates. Constant reminder of what she suffered there.

Stunned, I roll to my knees. Ladykiller presses the cold barrel of his rifle to my head.

Anita hunches. "Please. Please don't kill him."

Each soft plea hollows my gut.

Holy crap, I care about her, too. The woman who destroyed my encampment and killed my brother. I have to say something.

I swallow and manage a smile. "It's okay, Anita."

No it's not, you moron.

But somehow, it is.

Pain thuds into my temple.

Death comes quick.

31

Heaven appears to be some woman calling me a moron.

And a monster headache.

I blink stinging eyes open. A hammer pounds my skull from the inside, darkness flaring at each beat. Anita crouches over me, a fist pressed to her forehead.

"Are you—talking to me?" I croak. "Seems unfair."

She flinches, colour blooming in her cheeks. My stomach clenches and ends my enjoyment of her startled expression.

"Going to be sick."

I roll, losing my touch with reality for a minute. The wooziness settles and I vomit into the dirt, each heave sinking claws of agony into my temple.

I'm too weak and dizzy to be embarrassed.

Anita helps me drink some water and cradles my head in her lap, her fingers gloriously cool. A dressing pinches the skin at my temple.

We're alone on the track, no sign of the men.

Or what's left of them.

The world refuses to stop spinning.

"Oh god, what happened?" I say.

"What do you remember?"

"The soldiers. Taking our weapons. You."

Her gaze darts away but her hands continue to stroke me. "Are they dead?"

She nods, still not looking at me.

Of course they are. Four muscled he-men with rifles against one slim woman.

Is there anyone who attacks her and lives?

Yeah, me and John Anders, the dickhead.

I grip her fluttering hand and press it over my chest. Her eyes meet mine, wide and scared.

"When do I get to rescue you? This is very hard on the ego." I manage a smile, my quivering muscles not fully cooperative. "And why does no one want to kidnap me for nefarious sexual purposes? Aren't I pretty?"

Her breath hitches and she tugs on her hand.

Trying to hide.

I refuse to let go.

She can break free but only if she hurts me.

A single tear glistens on her cheek and I capture it on a fingertip.

"You really care about me," I say.

She shakes her head, her hair covering her face. "I need you for the warships."

"Is that all?"

"And the sex. Definitely the sex."

I smirk. "Still fighting me, my beautiful, stubborn warrior."

"We should get out of here," she says in a rush. "Can you stand?"

Man, she's even sexier when she's flustered. I could tease her more but fainting seems a possibility and I want us to be somewhere safe.

She pulls me gently to my feet, hovering while I sway and

blink to banish the sparkles in my eyeballs. I concentrate on not puking and Anita leaves my side long enough to dig something from the rucksack. Flapping hands stop her from jamming a tablet down my throat.

"Jesus, woman, I can take a pill. I'm not an invalid."

She retreats, fiddling with our weapons. She has everything the soldiers took, including two of their rifles.

And not a scratch on her.

She hands me one of the SA80s. I adjust the sling to fit since I'm not a steroid-happy beefcake.

"Well, look at you, breaking hearts and kicking ass."

Okay, so I can tease her a bit more. I'm hurt, not dead.

She frowns, shouldering the rucksack. "You're babbling. The head injury must be worse than I thought."

"Ouch. Belittle the wounded guy."

I force myself to take a step. The movement sledgehammers into my skull. I channel my dignity, buried beneath the urge to clutch my head and weep. My boots slide through the dust, more zombie shuffle than walking, but it's a start. Anita matches my pace.

She probably thinks she's being subtle but the tense arms and twitching panic when I lurch give her away.

We make it about ten metres down the track before she trips on her own feet.

I snort. "Did they hit you on the head, too?"

"No," she snaps.

She scrambles upright and raises her chin, stalking ahead, dust sifting from her clothes. I grin and shamble in her wake.

Thankfully, we don't go far.

Anita turns off the track to follow a river and I smother my relief.

Staying vertical is difficult and the undulating terrain doesn't help.

Anita stops where the bank of slippery rock lowers close to the water, the trees crowding in. I swallow a groan and sink to the ground, my back propped against a trunk. Pain sizzles down my neck and jaw.

She cocks an eyebrow. "Thought you weren't an invalid."

"Don't want to stretch myself. Head injuries are serious, you know."

She expands the pod and sets up camp. I breathe and convince myself I don't need to vomit.

"Come on, sick boy, get in the pod."

Light voice, worried face.

I hold out my hands. She rolls her eyes but takes them and helps me to my feet. I step into her, partly to stop myself from crumpling but mostly because I want a hug.

My arms slide around her shoulders. "I like this caring side of you. Makes me feel all warm and fluffy."

I kiss her, meaning for it to be brief and reassuring but she moans, arching into me. Her fingers grip my hips, the kiss deepening.

Sex sounds great. I'm game.

If she doesn't mind me flitting in and out of consciousness.

She pulls away, her throat working. "You won't think that when I wake you every few hours."

I pause a second from recapturing her lips. "You're kidding."

"Am I? Get in the pod."

Muttering for appearances' sake, I climb in.

Lying down is wonderful. My body aches all over, my eyelids heavy.

Anita tucks me in but I'm too tired to grumble.

It's supposed to be me making her feel safe, not the other way around.

* * *

She wasn't kidding.

She wakes me every two hours to shine a light in my eyes and ask the same questions.

"What's your name? When's your birthday? What year is it?"

I humour her the first time. "Blake O'Riley. Twenty-second of June two thousand and five. Two thousand and forty."

"Happy birthday a week ago," she whispers in the dark.

"Not my best. Two months in no man's land. No cake or presents…"

Has it only been a week? A week since I ran out of bullets, contemplated suicide and threw myself on top of Anita.

Only one of those hasn't changed.

The second time, I mumble something that must be right as she lets me drift off. The third time, I say, "Baby, if you wake me again, you will regret it."

She chuckles, curled against my back. "Irritability is often a sign of worsening head trauma. Maybe I should wake you every hour to be safe."

I roll and pin her. The ground yaws a little but definitely not as bad, the pain dull. I nibble her jaw and her pulse leaps.

"Wake me and I will show no mercy. I wonder what else I can get you to tell me."

I move lower and kiss along her collarbone.

"Okay, I won't wake you again." She squirms, her voice shaking.

Afraid of what she'll say?

"No sex until you've recovered. Too strenuous."

I lick the pulsing hollow of her throat. "Like you would refuse me."

Her eyes glitter in the dark but I kiss her before she can growl at me.

Snarling predator to wanton hussy in one slide of my tongue.

"God, the way you react to me is just awesome."

"Yeah, yeah, you're beautiful and irresistible." She slaps my chest. "Now get off and go back to sleep."

I shift and pull her with me. She cuddles into my side.

"Are you in pain?" she says.

Drifting to sleep—relaxed, unguarded, concussed—I tell her the truth.

"Not anymore."

32

Anita's flailing arms jerk me awake, which does not soothe my fragile head. She whirls to me, clawing the hair from her eyes. I blink at her pale, panic-stricken face and coax my heart back to where it belongs.

"Christ, woman, I'm still alive. Calm down."

Her shoulders hunch, the colour rising in her cheeks. I sit up, my fingers itching to stroke the stubborn set of her jaw.

Her eyes narrow. "What are you grinning at?"

"You're being cute."

"This is not cute. It's ridiculous."

"Don't be so hard on yourself. You've already told me how great and beautiful I am."

She clenches her fist. "Stop laughing at me! This is all your damn fault."

"How is it my fault?"

Her mouth snaps shut and her gaze darts away.

Hell no. I can't return to her telling me nothing while she flounces around with her nose in the air.

We are way past that.

"Why did you beg for my life yesterday? Why does the thought of me dying make you cry?" I suck in a breath. "Why are you scared of me?"

"You already know. You don't have to fucking ask."

"I want to hear you say it."

"Fuck you."

I grin. "Soon. Tell me why first."

"You're a close friend."

"Nope. Try again."

"You're like a brother to me."

"Gross."

She snorts and claps a hand over her mouth.

"Fine," she mumbles. "I care about you, you insufferable asshole."

Not exactly hearts and flowers but sincere all the same.

"Does calling me names make you feel better?"

"Yes, it does, you dick."

I laugh and pain throbs from my temple. Anita force-feeds me another couple of ibuprofen.

"I need to change your bandage."

I nod and she peels the dressing off, cleaning the area with a lemon-scented antiseptic wipe. I try not to wriggle or whine.

Stoic. Like a man.

She brushes the hair out of my eyes, her fingers continuing on to tickle across my scalp. She catches me watching her and ducks her head, fumbling open a dressing packet. She smooths it on and strokes down my cheek. I capture her fingers.

"Still can't keep your hands to yourself. You going to take advantage of me while I'm injured?"

She smiles. "You wish."

"Oh, I do."

"You need to rest."

"I'll rest when I'm dead."

She force-feeds me real food next. I chew mechanically, still tired after a restless night and a rifle butt to the face. I don't argue when she shines her light in my eyes to check my pupils. I sigh instead of grinning like an idiot.

It's been a long time since someone took care of me.

* * *

I doze the rest of the day and sleep solidly all night. Feel almost normal by the morning. The pain is a low ache, the dizziness gone. But it takes until afternoon to convince Anita I'm well enough to move.

She worries about me. Really, properly worries about me.

I use my mother as an excuse for the haste. Lost son desperate to be reunited. It's true but I also want to get Anita out of Scotland before more arseholes try to abduct her.

I'm the only arsehole who gets to abduct her.

We abandon the trees and I take the lead for a couple of hours, my shoulders tense from the constant vigilance.

No more getting caught unawares by psychopaths.

We pass abandoned fields and crumbling villages. More fields.

"Oh, fuck, is that a weapon?" Anita says, peering between a gap in the hedge.

The centre of the field contains a black post, taller than us.

So much for my vigilance.

"If it was, we'd be dead already. There are tyre tracks leading up to it."

Anita edges closer and I follow, searching for movement in the field. She touches the thing then rubs her palm on her trousers.

"Whatever it is, it's goddamn creepy."

We leave it to perform its mystery function and hustle through a farmyard. I stop where the dusty track curves past a collapsing shed still sheathed in the hint of pig dung.

"What—"

"Listen," I say.

Anita cocks her head. The wind sighs, a loose board creaks. A muffled rumble and roar.

Her eyes widen. "Is that—"

"The edge of our world, baby."

It's a bit embarrassing I didn't think of it myself instead of stumbling around like a jackass, dehydrated and lost. Escape never crossed my mind. No long-term plan but grief.

Anita picks at the edge of the bandage on her forearm, her SA80 rifle hanging loose on its sling, the Glock at her hip. Armed but somehow vulnerable.

"What if their world is no more normal than ours? What if it's worse?" A quiet panic fills her face. "The radio broadcast my friend heard was two years ago and said something about New London. What if we get there and it's the same crap in a different country?"

I capture her hand and tug her close, brushing a strand of hair off her cheek. "It's not going to be worse. We would've heard something. Seen something."

"What if they're all dead?"

"There's no global catastrophe that would kill everyone else and leave us untouched. Someone's alive out there. We just need to find them."

Her palms stroke my chest, her fingertips playing along the dog-tags beneath my t-shirt. The light touch tingles to my stomach.

"How can you be an optimist *and* a romantic *and* have the

forgiveness of a saint?"

"Hey, you make me sound like a wimp. I can be wicked." I grip her hips, pressing her into me. "I can be bad."

I kiss her and her hands fist in my t-shirt, an eager noise in her throat. She rubs herself against my erection, her spine bowed, the taste of her thick on my tongue.

I need to get her naked, feel the electric slide of her skin on mine and bury myself—

I break the kiss, ridiculously breathless. "Dammit, woman. We shouldn't lower our guard now, this close to the end."

"I do believe you kissed me," she says in the haughty, husky voice that makes me want to bite her.

I manage to resist. "Come on. Let's go find out the state of the rest of the world."

Ignoring the curving path, I plunge into vegetation masking a smaller track. The swish of Anita's passage follows behind. Gulls call down by the sea, the sun baking the dusty grass.

"If they are normal, or at least civilised, what do you think they'll do to us?"

I stop myself from turning around, my eyes scanning the tangled hawthorn for flashes of colour and shadows that don't belong.

"Technically, we're still UK citizens. If we don't reach England, we'll be shipped there as soon as possible. I imagine there'll be a lot of questions and waiting around but if we both have living relatives, that's where they'll send us."

God, I hope my mum is alive. The reunion will be amazing and bittersweet and awful all rolled into one.

"You don't think they'll arrest us as war criminals?"

The path dips to hide us in a bowl of greenery. I halt Anita with my hands on her shoulders, my fingers splayed over the straps of the rucksack.

She refused to let me carry it on account of my head injury.

"We're not war criminals. *You're* not a war criminal."

She frowns at my chest. "Wilful killing, wanton destruction. Seems pretty criminal."

"Justified and proportional to what we deserved."

"You didn't deserve this," she whispers, raising her eyes, the sadness in them punching into my gut. "If it wasn't for me, you'd be in Livingston right now."

"Yeah, hiding from Wick and watching him enslave the world. Sounds great."

"You would've had Dylan." She ducks her head.

I tilt her chin until she looks at me, her pulse fluttering under my fingertips.

"But not my humanity." Don't say any more. "And not you."

For god's sake. When did I turn into a bubbling moron?

"I'm no great prize, not over family."

Jesus, she actually believes it. How can this beautiful, stubborn woman not know her own worth?

I hug her. Tentative hands slide around my waist to the small of my back.

"Then you don't see yourself."

Like I do.

Well, look at that. I can be a proper man and censor myself instead of blurting everything out.

What the hell am I doing? I've gotten too comfortable with her in the intense week we've been together. Distance will be healthy. She'll go to Kent—or New Kent or whatever—I'll go to Ireland and my damn skin will settle down. Not to mention the weird things she does to my stomach.

Crap.

I definitely need some distance.

33

The bowl of land terminates in a field of reeds taller than our heads. They sway in the wind, the stalks and leaves a forest of yellow and green. The crash of the sea swells somewhere on the other side.

A shiver of unease dances up my spine. Claustrophobic, who me? It seems stupid to spend half an hour finding another way around instead of two minutes thrashing through the dust and gloom.

I tighten my hands on my rifle and push into the wall of heat, the air almost too solid to breathe. Dried mud cracks under my boots in little plumes. The reeds are dying, their musky, fishy odour catching in the back of my throat. I increase my pace, the crunch and rustle drowning out the waves on the beach. Grit stings my eyes and coats my mouth, powdering my navy t-shirt.

Anita finally took it off. It smells like her. Bewitching, distracting. Good enough to eat.

Will you focus on getting her to safety, not on humping her every two seconds?

I shake my head and nearly slice my eyeball on one of the stiff leaves.

I like sex as much as the next guy but this is getting ridiculous.

The cloying shade lightens, a puff of salt-laden air banishing the staleness. The reeds wither to brown on the edge and shrink into the dirt, petering into bright green grass stretching to sand dunes and bristling bushes.

I turn to Anita.

She isn't there.

Hello, panic.

I open my mouth to call her name and gunfire rattles in the depths of the reeds. Ice solidifies in my stomach.

"Anita!"

I dive into the whispering stalks, my rifle barrel batting them out of the way.

Have Unification Army found us again? Or is it a scabby Borderlander far from home?

You goddamn moron. If she's dead—

She's not dead. She's indestructible, a warrior. She protects me better than I do her. I'll find her, our enemies scattered at her feet, and she'll smirk at me for being slow. I'll scoop her in my arms and never let her go. I'll—

I stumble to a halt, my rifle butt bruising my shoulder. Anita dangles from the mouth of a huge snake, the rucksack lodged between its fangs. It shakes its wedge-shaped head, whipping her legs through the reeds.

The biggest abomination I've ever seen.

"Blake—shoot—it!" she yells, her arms pinned by the straps of the rucksack, her body jerking at each shake of the snake's head.

She curls her knees to her chest. I suck in a breath to steady my trembling hands. My burst of bullets thunks into the beast's creamy belly, mangling scales and exposing pink flesh.

The shriek it makes scares me worse than being alone in

a room with Wick, though the cold, reptilian intelligence reminds me of him.

The snake tosses its head, the rucksack slipping free, and Anita vanishes into the reeds. I take a step towards her. The creature rears, thick blood darkening its belly.

I plant my feet, my fingers blanched on my rifle. "You want her, you bitch, you go through me."

The snake lunges, its dripping fangs as long as my arm. I roll in a cloud of dust and rustling leaves. The SA80 slaps my shoulder. A glittering, orange-gold eye fixes on me. Its mouth opens, a grey tongue tasting the air. Tasting me. I squeeze the trigger until my rifle clicks empty. The abomination attacks.

Jesus, how is it alive?

I straighten my left arm and flick my wrist, the trigger of the electrigun sliding into my hand. My fingers clench on the bulb. A crackling bolt of electricity ripples over glistening scales but the thing still barrels closer, the dark tunnel of its throat widening to swallow me. Bullets patter into its side.

Anita, her feet shoulder width apart, hair falling over her face, her teeth bared. Furious green eyes glare at the snake, blood welling from scratches on her arms and mixing with the dust.

Relief weakens my knees.

She's okay.

Another ball-shrivelling screech comes from the snake. Its body blocks the sun and throws me in shadow, ruby droplets splattering the reeds. My hand spasms on the trigger of the electrigun. The bolt connects but the abomination drops its head and slams its blunt nose into my chest. The force catapults me backwards. My breath explodes out, my ribs surely pulverised.

The last thing I see in the whirl of yellow and green is the snake stretched out flat. Unmoving.

Thank god. I've finally managed to save Anita. My ego can rest in peace.

I hit the ground. *Hard.*

34

I don't lose consciousness. Probably a good thing considering how much of a battering my brain has already taken. I lie on my back, my eyes squeezed shut, and coax my lungs into breathing tiny sips of burning air.

Is this how Dylan felt in his final moments?

I swallow a groan and fist my hand in the dirt. A clatter of bullets makes me jump and almost pass out.

If it's Anita finishing the snake, I'm still taking it as a win. If it's someone else attacking us, I hope they hurry up and shoot me.

I focus every molecule on lying as motionless as possible to stop myself from whimpering.

It would undermine my tough, manly exterior.

A weight thuds to the ground next to me, all hitching breath and fluttering hands.

Do I look dead?

I want to open my mouth and tell her I'm okay but fear blood may bubble out. Maybe my ribs are poking through my chest.

Lie still and breath is about all I can do without sobbing.

"I love you," Anita whispers. "Please don't die."

My heart freezes then thuds against my aching ribs, snapping my eyes open. The sky wobbles, my woozy head not helped by the swaying reeds.

Oh god, don't faint. She'll pass it off as a dream. Lie to protect herself. She's been doing it this whole time.

Cares about me, my arse. She—

Sweet-holy-Jesus. I have to hear it again. Maybe I imagined it. I'm not exactly at my most lucid.

Anita kneels at my side, her head bowed, fingers fumbling for my pulse. I capture her shaking hand and she gasps, jerking backwards to sit hard on her arse. Startled eyes meet mine, her face pale beneath the streaks of yellowed dust.

"What did you say?"

Hey, I can talk. Maybe my ribs are only broken in a thousand places, not pulverised.

The familiar flustered panic colours her cheeks. Her gaze zips around the whispering reeds as if looking for an escape route.

It's far too late for that.

Good god, how has this happened?

"I…" Her mouth works. "Don't die?"

She hides behind her hair but the tumble of gold can't save her.

"Before that."

"Nothing. You must have hallucinated."

I shove up on my elbows. My ribs politely ask what the hell I think I'm doing. I groan and flop back down.

"Anita, tell me what you said."

She shakes her head, frowning at her knees. "Nothing. Babbling, as usual. Ignore me."

"*Coward.*"

Her head snaps up, a snarl twisting her lips.

From vulnerable to furious in one nanosecond.

I smirk at her and she flushes, dropping her eyes. I tangle my fingers in her hair.

"Look at me! Look at me and tell me what you said."

"No. Let go of me or, I swear to god, I will punch you right in the chest."

I laugh and immediately regret it. "You won't hurt me. You can't."

"Can. Already have." She holds a trembling fist above my ribs. "Let me go. *Now.*"

I place my hand over hers, pretending she's the only one who's shaking, and lower it gently towards my chest.

"What are you doing?" she squeaks.

God, she's cute. Squirming and nervous under my touch. Stronger than anyone I know despite being beaten and broken by the worst of people, her shields built from suffering and blood. I love the snootiness that hides a core of tenderness and innocence only I get to see. She humbles me. Dazzles me.

Oh, wow. This is new.

Her hand settles on my chest.

I can't tell if I'm breathless from the pain or my pounding heart.

The simple words catch in my throat. I've never said them before to anyone other than family.

I swallow. "I love you, too, you idiot."

Yup, I'm definitely a romantic.

"That's not what I said," she yelps.

Try again without the name-calling, you jackass.

"I love you," I say.

Her body wriggles beside me but her hand stays perfectly still on my chest.

"Stop it," she pants, her hair sticking to her flushed face. "You don't. You can't."

I roll my eyes.

Of course she fights me.

"Why?" I say. "Because you killed my brother?"

"Why the hell else? I murdered what might be the last of your family."

"It wasn't murder, Anita. We've spent years slaughtering each other. Fight or die, you know that."

"Fine. Confuse me with logic. What if we escape and your mother's alive? You going to introduce me? Tell her how Dylan died?"

"Yes."

Holy crap, I want to introduce her to my mother.

Anita snorts. "Don't be ridiculous. She'd hate me and be upset with you."

"She'd forgive you, like I have. You've suffered enough. It was my fault. Our fault—Nationless. This is our punishment and we deserve it."

She shakes her head, always so quick to defend me even against myself. I drag her closer. She growls and I can't stop a grin.

"You really are scared."

"I'm not scared."

There's the pout I know and… love.

I reel her in. She doesn't struggle, bracing her free hand on the ground, her other hand scorching my chest and doing crazy things to my stomach.

Now I know the reason.

"This is why you cry every time I get hurt. Why you begged for my life. Why you can't control yourself around me." I release her hair to cup her head. "You love me."

Try not to sound so awe-struck, you douche, grumbles my ego.

"I don't," she whispers against my mouth, her eyes wide.

"Liar."

I kiss her, a teasing glide of lips. She whimpers and climbs into my lap.

Her body can't hide how she feels, even if she's too afraid to say it.

My hands drop to her glorious ass. She holds her weight off me, the effort quivering through her arms. I thrust my hips into her, my erection straining against my combats.

I want to make love to her.

Make love? Jesus, it's what I've been doing this whole time. I fell for her as soon as she trembled underneath me and begged me to touch her.

She collapses into me, a moan in her throat. I can't mask a grimace as she crushes my chest.

She jerks upright. "Shit! I'm sorry. Wait, no. It's your fault."

"Sure, blame the injured guy," I groan. "I think my ribs are pulverised."

"You got to rescue me for once and already with the complaints."

She crawls off and eases me into a sitting position, patting the dust from my t-shirt while I try not to whine about it.

"Turns out it's not as fun as I imagined."

"Did you lose consciousness? Do you feel dizzy? Nauseated?" She squints at me, probably checking my pupils.

I have to admire her bravado. Gamely switching the subject to my health.

I grab her hand before she can peel my eyelids up.

"I'm fine—winded. No need to quiz me on what year it is. And you know I didn't lose consciousness. I heard what you said."

No escaping the truth, baby.

If I have to face it, so does she.

She squirms and I tuck her hair behind her ear, trailing my fingers along the mulish thrust of her jaw.

"I love you, Anita."

"No, you don't."

God, she's adorable. How can this stunning, passionate, honourable woman believe she isn't good enough to be loved? A disarming insecurity. How can anyone know her and not love her?

I grip her arms and shake her. Gently. "I love you, you stubborn, mouthy, pain in the arse."

She fights a smile and opens her mouth, no doubt to argue, but I've had enough. Incurable romantic that I am, I kiss her to shut her up.

35

Two seconds of kissing and Anita starts taking my clothes off.

"Need to assess—your ribs for damage," she pants.

Oh yeah, she can't get enough.

Her fingers stroke my chest, following the beaded chains of my dog-tags to a large, reddened mark where the snake hit me.

"No fair. I can't undress you." I flick one strap of the rucksack.

"Safer that way."

The growl slips out but it's worth the dazed look on her face. She scrabbles at the button of my combats, yanking the zip and gripping my cock in one hand. My eyes roll back in my head.

Okay, this will be fast, the pressure in my balls building from one squeeze of her fingers. I'll make up for it in round two. Then I can take my time and tease her until she squirms and moans and tells me she loves me.

God, I am so close to coming. The woman destroys my self-control.

I fucking love it.

A low hiss shivers from the reeds and dumps a bucket of ice on my excitement. Anita leaps to her feet, her Glock raised and sweeping the crumpled mess of vegetation surrounding

211

us. The wind sighs through the stalks, the only snake the one we've left bleeding on the ground, its head a fleshy pulp.

"Jesus-fucking-Christ," Anita gasps, holstering her gun. "We should get out of here."

I nod, zipping myself up and climbing to my feet. I fake a stumble and she darts to my side. My hand in her hair captures her, the other on her hip.

"Clumsy me," I say, and grin.

Hey, I've had a fright, I'm not dead. I very much want to get back to what we were doing.

Her fingers trail up my spine, sending tingles to the tip of my erection.

I nibble her pouting mouth. "Let's set up the pod."

"The pod? But the warships—"

"Will wait." I pull her head back, exposing her throat to my lips. "If I'm going to make love to you, I want to do it right. To tease you, oh so slowly, until you tell me what I want to hear."

"Blake…"

I sink my teeth into her thudding, throbbing pulse and she moans.

"Such a wanton little hussy," I chuckle into her neck.

I release her and she staggers.

Putty in my hands.

Her face flushes but she scowls, lobbing my t-shirt at me. Laughing, I catch it and slip it on. She tosses her empty rifle next to mine while I dust myself down and confirm my ribs are badly bruised, not broken. The electrigun rattles on my left arm, jagged cracks splitting the casing.

"Damn. I liked this thing." I jiggle my arm and something inside the weapon tinkles. "I think it took the brunt of the impact."

Anita unstraps the electrigun and cradles it in her hands, her eyes sad, before she lets it drop to the dirt.

"Promise me you won't die," she says in a tiny voice, her gaze fixed on the broken weapon.

I stop myself from blurting it out.

Any promise I make is one I can't break. Dylan's death taught me that.

My finger traces Anita's cheekbone, the ache in my chest nothing to do with my battered ribs. "Baby, you know I can't promise you that."

"No. *No.* You can't make me—feel this much and then—die."

"Still can't say it? That's okay. You will."

"You arrogant bas—"

I crush her mouth to mine, my fingers buried in her hair. She sobs low in her throat and clings to me, showing me how she feels better than any words. I hold her at arm's length before I do something embarrassing. Like cry.

Speaking takes a couple of attempts. "I promise I'll try my fucking hardest *not* to die."

The tension in her face eases.

On this, she believes me.

I'll work on the rest.

* * *

We expand the pod on the landward side of a sand dune, sheltered by bushes and bathed in the sweet coconut smell of their flowers. The rumble of the surf grounds me as I lower Anita to the covers, her eyes raw and vulnerable and stripped of all defences. I undress her as if it's our first time.

In a way, it is.

I trap her wandering hands before they can distract me. "Let me prove how I feel."

And I do, though it takes every bit of my tattered self-control to keep it gentle and slow. She trembles underneath me. Moans my name, over and over, like a prayer. Her tears captivate me and mark me as hers. I kiss the salt from her cheeks and cup her face.

"I love you, Anita."

"I love you, Blake," she says, "you bastard."

A ridiculous grin stretches my face. I circle my hips just to watch her writhe.

"Oh, woman, what you do to me. You and that mouth."

She wraps herself around me, drowning my senses in her scent and heat. The tenderness unmans me. The desperate desire to hold her and never let go is strong enough to hurt, even though I'm buried inside her.

I tangle my fingers in her hair and pretend it's her tears on my cheeks. "Say it again."

She pouts but one thrust of my hips has her eyes rolling back.

"Blake—"

"Say it."

"I love you, dammit."

"Without the cursing."

I nibble her throat, easing myself in and out of her in an excruciating rhythm that slowly drives me crazy. The agonising restraint is worth the frantic thudding of her pulse and the wild light in her eyes.

She is so close to surrendering.

I raise up on my elbows to look at her and condemn myself further. Tears glitter in her lovely eyes, her face flushed and glowing, lips half-parted. Her hair frames the glorious curves of her body and sticks to her dewed skin.

"I love you," she says.

I smirk. "Damn right you do."

36

Everything will be okay in the end. How can it not? Anita survived worse to get this far, what's a little warship theft and desertion compared to that? We'll make it to the outside world and be reunited with our families. I'll meet her parents. Introduce her to my mother with the unvarnished, brutal and glorious truth.

Typical couple stuff.

We'll find somewhere to be normal together. No more factions or war or killing, just me and her. A nice soft bed for her to moan my name in, her body arching on the sheets, slick and wet and glowing—

Crap. Must stop doing that.

A quiet celebration will honour each anniversary of Dylan's death. Maybe I'll return to the ruins of my home and the grave of my brother when the fighting finally ends. Retrace my desperate journey through no man's land. Eat a butterfly or two. I'll finish in the place it began with Anita.

In the crumbling old farmhouse where she surrendered.

And where the last soldier of Nationless fell.

Let Me Know What You Think!

Thank you for reading my book! I love hearing from my readers so please leave me a review.

Can't wait to hear from you!

For a free prequel to *The Faction War Chronicles,* you can also join my mailing list at nadinelittle.com/free-prequel by scanning the QR code below:

Buy the Finale: *Homecoming*
Why did the rest of the world fall silent? And will Anita ever find her place in it?

About the Author

Nadine Little lives in Scotland and is an ecologist with an interest in botany. She writes science fiction and fantasy in her spare time when she's not reading or playing *Fortnite* on her PlayStation.

The year 2020 seemed the perfect time to publish her debut trilogy *The Faction War Chronicles* since it all went to hell. Sometimes she worries that people will look at her differently.

But not really.

You can connect with me on:
- https://nadinelittle.com
- https://twitter.com/Nadine_Little_
- https://www.facebook.com/nadinelittleauthor

Subscribe to my newsletter:
- https://nadinelittle.com/free-prequel